Wicked Girls

STEPHANIE HEMPHILL

Wicked Girls

A NOVEL OF THE SALEM WITCH TRIALS

BALZER + BRAY
An Imprint of HarperCollins*Publishers*

Balzer + Bray is an imprint of HarperCollins Publishers.

Wicked Girls: A Novel of the Salem Witch Trials
www.harperteen.com

Library of Congress Cataloging-in-Publication Data
is available.
ISBN 978-0-06-185328-9 (trade bdg.) —
ISBN 978-0-06-185329-6 (lib. bdg.)

Typography by Ray Shappell
10 11 12 13 14   CG/RRDB   10 9 8 7 6 5 4 3 2 1
❖
First Edition

For Alessandra

THE GIRLS

in order of appearance

MERCY LEWIS *(age 17)* is an orphan of the French and Indian War. She is a new servant in Thomas Putnam's house.

MARGARET WALCOTT *(age 17)* is Ann Putnam Jr.'s step-cousin (because Margaret's father married Thomas Putnam's sister, Deliverance, after Margaret's mother died). She comes from a lower social status than her younger cousin.

ANN PUTNAM JR. *(age 12)* is Thomas Putnam's eldest child and therefore a young lady with stature in Salem Village.

BETTY PARRIS *(age 8)* is the daughter of Reverend Samuel Parris and Abigail Williams's cousin. She is the youngest of the accusers.

ABIGAIL WILLIAMS *(age 12)* is a niece of Reverend Samuel Parris and a cousin to Betty Parris. She lives at the parsonage with the Reverend and his family. She is one of the first seers.

ELIZABETH HUBBARD *(age 17)* is another new girl in Salem Village who has been sent to live with Doctor Griggs and his wife. She is a distant niece of the Doctor. Doctor Griggs is her grandparents' age.

SUSANNAH SHELDON *(age 18)* is the only girl not from Salem Village, but from Salem Town instead. She serves in William Shaw's house. She joins the group last.

SALEM
January 1692

Silent, not even the twitter
of insects. The wind stills
against a distant sky of clouds.
The cold is gray and fierce,
bitter as a widow at the grave.
The trees' bare bony fingers
point crookedly
toward Heaven or Hell
or worse than that, toward nowhere.

Winter days
wear long as the ocean shore,
governed by a god
harsher than windstorm hail
and more punishing than the waves
that break ships in two.

There are rules to follow here,
one righteous path
thrashed down through the woods.

GIRL

Mercy Lewis, 17

Before the orange of dawn
before the hearth fire's lit
when the kitchen floor
will feel as ice under my boots
and I would rather keep under quilt,
my eyelids sealed,
my nightclothes neck-tight;
he slobbers kisses on my cheek,
his gritty tongue
swabs my chin
like a wet woolen stocking.

"Wilson." I whisper and try not to giggle.
With two paws on the bed
he licks my hand.
"Down, boy. Don't wake the baby."
Wilson bobs his head,
sits silent as the dark.
I splash water, button clothes,
and slip quickly into the black of day.

Like I be blind, Wilson guides me
to the place where he can be fed.
"Go on then, eat,"
I say, and point at the bowl.

He just grins his five teeth.
He hangs his front paws on my shoulders.
My arms wrap around him.
I ruffle his gold, dank fur.

The sun flashes through the window.
"Come, boy!" Mister Putnam calls.
Wilson's ears perk and he is off
as after a doe, down the hall heavy
and loud-pawed. The baby cries.

"Girl!"
The voice commands
like a great fist
pounding the wall.

CAST TO SALEM VILLAGE
Mercy Lewis, 17

"Mercy, bring this wool
to the weaver," Missus orders.
I bundle the yarns
under my cloak.
I feel as though I've been thrown
to an ocean of ice floes,
the weather so flays my skin
and gnaws at my bones.

I hand the weaver's son
the yarns to dye.
"What a pretty cloth
for such a pretty one," he says.
His eyes tighten upon me
like a corset.
"'Tis not for me," I say,
and turn to leave.
He catches me by the shoulder,
his hand stained indigo.
"Did one ever tell thee
thou hast bluest eyes?"

"Jonathan!" His father rumbles
right as a reverend.
"Thou art needed to mix the dye."

Jonathan boy scurries off.
But his father looms down on me,
tries to stare me apart
like I be one of the dock girls
flashing stockings and crinoline.
Without a flinch, I gather my scarf
and push back into the freeze.

Even in deep winter
the town of Salem swells.
The port fills with merchandise,
and pockets droop heavy with pounds.
On the barge, bags of grain
and jugs of cider unload,
for the Salem Village farms
see meager crops.

I am told the slaves used to eat pudding
at Thomas Putnam's table,
but not in a winter this cold.
Few in Reverend Parris's flock
dine far above broth and grain.

I meet the eyes
of a uniformed soldier.
I cannot praise and bow.
The wars up north
echo in my skull
like the sea inside a shell.

A different kind of battle bruises
Salem's shores.
For here neighbor to neighbor,
brother to kin,
old money against the new,
jealous feuds
whistle through the night.

And I have barely a bonnet
to protect my head.
Why, Lord? Why am I here?

STEP-COUSIN

Margaret Walcott, 17

Sky's painful bright outside
the parsonage, even without sun.
I scratch the wet topping my hood
and sneeze. "Hole in the roof
been dripping me in meeting.
I fear I caught the cough," I say to Ann.

"Perhaps tomorrow at our gathering
we'll find you a remedy." Ann smiles.
She turns her head from me
and stares dumb-like at her new servant girl.

I shake and spit up a cough and a sneeze
what pierce the ears
like a horsewhip cracking.
Folk turn and stare.
I whisper, "Ann, have you a kerchief?
I must be looking all spotted and ugly."

Ann shakes her head no
and steps back from me.
"You know you always look fair."
She pulls her cloak tighter
round her shoulders.

My nose be dripping worse than the roof.
I need to wipe it on my glove.
I sniffle.

Break in morning service be at an end
and brethren file toward the meeting door.
"Wait, and we'll go in after the others."
I hold Ann's arm, but she wiggles free.

"Mother said I must not dawdle
outside meeting." Ann shrugs
and darts toward church.

When all's gone into the meetinghouse
or be looking that way,
I turn myself back
toward the parsonage.
I swipe back and forth
my nose 'pon my sleeve
till my cuff be wet as my head.

I look up,
and he stares on me.
I want to crawl under my skirt.

His shoulders be broad
as a boat's bow.
I feel cherry-cheeked.
Will he tell I be not a lady?

He walks toward me.
I see now 'tis worse
than I did think.
He is not my elder.
"Isaac Farrar—"
I cough and the tears
brim my eyes.
Oh, I will be always
the girl who uses her sleeve.
"It be not . . ." "I meant but to . . ."
I wince at the thought
of his scold or laugh.

Only three feet from my own,
Isaac just smiles.
And not like some snake in low grass,
but a smile like warm,
sweet milk.

I turn away quick
and stumble over my own foot
as I run direct into church.

THE WAY WE ARE SEATED
Margaret Walcott, 17

"Life is not for joy and jolly,
  but for toil and test,
  an order ordained."
Reverend rings in our ears.
The men of land and money
lined up front
like a fence of wood stakes.
My father snug among them
what serve on town council
and vote as church members.
After Mother died, Father sold his cargo ship,
built the biggest house in the Village
and wed the sister of Thomas Putnam
to sit on that bench where he does.

Behind my father, the men
of mended trousers
straighten their necks.
I try never to stare
directly at the upright heads
of those what sit behind—
the good sons, all them
not off or lost to war.
My eyes shift 'pon Isaac.
Did he just glance this way?

Nothing best smudge my face.
My hands heat under my gloves.
A drop of water dins my head
and I swallow hard a cough
screaming at the roof of my throat.

I switch fast my gaze
to the row below Isaac,
where sit the Gospel women,
which my father
wishes *me* to be.
Following the wives
of upstanding men
fall the lesser women,
and I sit behind them, us girls
and servants. The slaves and heathens
are not allowed
in church at all.

MERCY LEWIS

Ann Putnam Jr., 12

Her name is a blessing,
not simple and plain like Ann.
Ann with sticky spiderweb hair,
not the gold that willows
down Mercy's back, smooth
and perfect as God's breath.
All the men stop
whatever they are about
whenever she goes past.

HELPFUL
Ann Putnam Jr., 12

"Mercy, let me help you
carry the other bucket,"
I say, and sidle next to her on the path.
We walk along in silence.
I want to ask her how she slept,
what it was like when she lived in Maine,
did she have a horse,
did she see any Indians,
does she like me?
But instead I ask,
"Is Mother well this morning?"

Mercy doesn't even turn to look at me.
"Yea, she seems quite herself."
Mercy sets down her bucket,
rubs her hands together.

"I can carry both buckets if you like," I say.

She shrugs and smooths her bonnet.

I walk a step behind her
all the way home,
just so I can watch
the way she swings her arms.

A KIN TO WHOM?
Mercy Lewis, 17

Two weeks in this new place,
and night comes restless
with wind that claws
over the roof
like trapped cat paws.

When I close my eyes to sleep
I see my mother.
She holds my father's scalp.
Mouths of my sisters and brothers
gash open in scream.
Yet I hear no cry, no yell, nothing.

Under the bed, I pressed
my hands against my ears.
Bare Indian feet pounded
the floor, blood splattered
like a bucket of paint
hurled against the wall.
Blood raindrops fell
thick as mud, slow as dew.

As before, I cannot budge.
My legs dead wood.
I cannot lift my finger,
cannot blink an eye.
I do not think I breathe.
Like twisted wind
I hear the heavy breath
of the man who slays my mother.

I clasp my hands and pray
that this is just night sleep
and come morrow
I will be with my family.
But I wake in servant's quarters
under a thin quilt warmed by low fire,
rise to another day of fetching
for Missus Putnam and her babies.
Still I welcome the dawn.

NEVER LEFT ALONE

Mercy Lewis, 17

Little Ann circles, buzzes
in my ear like a barnyard fly.
I should almost like to shoo her
off my shoulder, but she fixes on me
with those chestnut eyes
like I were her queen.

"Let me put the baby to nap."
Ann relieves my arms.

Master Putnam shakes open the door,
a gust of wind shoots snow
behind his head like a fountain.
He staggers to his chair.
I untie his boots, yank free
his gloves and rub his red hands
to salve his numb and cold.
His eyes, like a flaming torch,
search over my body,
and I want to be anywhere
but bent at his feet.
Will this new man I serve
be the same as the last?

Wilson barks and shakes madly
his fur so that I am blanketed in white.
Master Putnam withdraws his hands,
"Go and fetch thee some dry clothes."

My heart ceases panic
as I turn the corner to my room.

"Why are you covered in snow?"
Ann startles me, then gallops to my side.

I point at the dog.

"Well, you had better change
to dry skirts," Ann says.

"Thank you, Ann.
I had not thought of that."

Ann blushes. She tags behind me
with a strange eagerness to help me
be rid of my soggy clothes.

I prevent her entering my room.
"Do you not have your gathering
and visit the Minister's girls today?
Should you not like to find
your cloak and gloves,
and then I will say you are at the stables?"

Ann sprouts up on her toes.
"Oh, yes! I shall find them."

I close my door, but a whine
and a scratch, and the door is wide again.
"Well then, dear Wilson, my prince,
in with thee."

LITTLE-GIRL GAMES
Margaret Walcott, 17

"I refuse playing at Scotch-hoppers."
I roll my eyes at little Betty.
"I did not sneak away
to play them baby games."

Abigail punches her younger cousin
in the side. "That be a game
for warm weather."

Ann paces the floor.
Her eyes fire.
"We could play Queen
and her subjects!"

"Fine. I be the Queen," I say.
"I command ye all
to sit under the table
and speak not at all."

The three little girls scurry
beneath the table like rabbits
scared into a hole.

I kick up my feet
and fluff my long black hair
in the hand glass. If only
my nose were not so red.

"What now?" Betty asks
after several minutes of quiet.

"You lose!" Abigail laughs.

"Silence!" I hold up my hand.
"You both lose. Stand in the corner."

The girls' eyes edge with tears.

Ann crawls from under the table.
"This is dull. Let's play at something new."

"This game be fine." I smile at her.

"We can tell fortunes." Ann dangles
my favorite before me.

Betty shakes her head.
"But that be a sin."

Ann whispers, "Not if none
does catch us."

I frown as they gather
a glass of water and four eggs.

"Do we form a circle?" Abigail asks
as though she's never done this.

I sneeze and my nose does drip.
I lift an arm to swipe it dry
and Isaac Farrar
with his wide shoulders and buttery smile
jumps into my thoughts.
My stomach squirms—
what a *fool* I acted,
rubbing my nose on my sleeve
in front of him!
I shake my head.

"What then do we do?" Abigail asks.

"Oh, *you* are a *fool*," I say,
and grab the bowl of eggs.

THE SHELL GAME
Ann Putnam Jr., 12

We huddle near the fire.
I clutch Betty Parris's little hand,
and she clasps Abigail.
Whether it was Margaret or me
or the Minister's niece
who first learned to read
egg whites in a glass, I know not.

Margaret cups an egg over the water,
then sets it down and says,
"Go on, Ann, let ye take the first egg."

I crack the shell, scoop out its yolk,
and ask what husband I will make.

We stare at the floating mass
as if it were a cloud,
and wager at the shape.

"It looks like a ship.
See the mast," Margaret says.
Betty nods.

"A sailor for Ann?" Abigail says,
  pawing for her own egg.
  I snatch the lot away.

"Or a royal or merchantman," I say,
  and hand the next fortune to Betty.

NOT MINE TO TAKE
Mercy Lewis, 17

I sneak from my work
of spinning and darning
and unlatch the wooden box
wherein hides the necklace
too lavish to be worn upon the neck.

My fingers brush each red stone
of Missus Putnam's necklace,
a necklace that belonged
to her grandmother before her.
It will one day belong to little Ann.
The weight of the gems
clasps heavy round my neck.
In the looking glass
I turn side and side.
The stones change hue
in differing light.
I used to bounce sun
around the room
with my mother's hand mirror,
back when my greatest duties
were learning Mother's recipes
and writing out my passages.

How I despised that endless
copy work and now
what I would not give
to be a lady of correspondence
courted by suitors.

A flicker in the doorway.
I stuff the rubies and gold
deep into the box.
I fall to my knees
as though absorbed in housework.
The baby screams
and the kettle sirens,
and today I miss my mother
and her gentle smile
so far down inside me
I can barely drag myself
up off the floor.

CAUGHT
Margaret Walcott, 17

Past the crooked evergreen
and the brook what lost its water,
on my way home from playing
games on who'll make me husband,
I cross Ipswich Road.
I rub my eyes. His two blue ones
be looking straight on me.

My pulse starts to gallop
like a steed. But today I trip not.
I track on up to him and say,
"Be you following me?"

His arms be thick enough
to lift the axe of three men.
Isaac's laughter shakes
through him so fierce
it scatters the snow off his boots.
"Yea, Margaret Walcott,
betwixt tending the stables,
staking out the fields
and bringing wares to town,
I be scouting all the time after you."
He raises one brow.
"But where hast thou been?"

The color splashes over me,
drenching me red. I hold up my buckets.
"Fetching water," I say.

"Thou art far from any stream
I know of," Isaac says,
and shakes his head.
His eyes catch on me
like he be holding lightly
my face with his hand.

"I must then be lost," I say,
and I pick up my bucket
and my skirts and trot off.
And do so quite a bit like a lady.

ANN PUTNAM SR.

Ann Putnam Jr., 12

Mother never questions where
I have been. She notices not my entrance
into the house. But I note each patter of her foot.

She treadles the spinning wheel
as though she weaves a song
of high tempo. I am mesmerized.

I set to work at her feet.
My hands sting just from drafting her wool.

"There are too many loose fibers."
Her voice is a whip.

I rub harder the flax between my hands
till the strands be perfect for the wheel.
Mother thanks me not.

"Will you teach me your way
to treadle?" I ask.
But Mother hears me not.

She hears only her own tapping
of the wheel.

She admires her yarn, refastens her bun
and motions me away.
"Go back to your study."

GIRLS AT PLAY?

Ann Putnam Jr., 12

I check again that we are alone
and crack open the eggshell.
Today what floats to the surface
is shaped like a death box.

I shudder, and we all drop hands.

Perhaps we should have sewn tapestry
or rolled hoops, instead of playing folk magic.

"Maybe your husband will be an undertaker,"
Abigail says.

But a chill colder than winter wind
trembles my arms. I hold in my breath.

Margaret's face turns dust and ice.
She says, "I fear we let loose
a thing what leads to the grave."

NOT SUPPOSED TO CONGREGATE
Margaret Walcott, 17

Reverend hands my father
the blue shawl I left
at the parsonage
like some one-eyed fool.
"The girls were
at some sort of mischief
at the meetinghouse.
Betty and Abigail been struck
rightful ill.
Pity Margaret can't act a lady
such as does her cousin Ann,"
Reverend Parris lectures to Father.
I can feel the leather lash my back
before Father closes the door.
If only they knew Ann
be not only with us
but be always first
with the herbs and chants and telling stones.

While I be strapped
it seems rightful unfair
that Ann be sainted.

I nearly wish to confess
what mischief we *all* been about,
conjuring that death box.
I swipe the tears from under my nose.

Step-Mother creaks afore my door
on her stubby legs.

"Maaaargaret!"
She stretches my name
like it were a hide.
"Be at your chores!"

The mound of mending in my basket
and bruises on my knees
from scouring like our maid
cause me ponder whether
I have enough merriment
with them little girls.

Outside the window
snow falls light and graceful
and perfect,
long as none does touch it.

Isaac must be riding
through this snow,
it covering his arms
and his head all white.
All them soft little flakes
landing 'pon his lips.
I touch my own
and wish to be out of here.

UPROOTED
Mercy Lewis, 17

I am no gypsy.
I seek but soil
and a place to dry my boots.

The boots I am given
at the Putnams' flap
as I walk.
My toes cannot fill them.
I swaddle my feet in muslin,
pack them to size.
But the stuffing shifts
for the boots are borrowed,
were never intended mine.

A sole stalk that survived
the cruelest winter, I search
for friendly, familiar terrain,
where I can fashion my boots
and trade in the temporary,
a plot of land
where my feet burrow
into the ground
and belong.

GREETINGS
Mercy Lewis, 17

Girl just my height
comes rapping on the door.
I've the littlest propped on my hip,
dirt on my apron and sleep
pasted beneath my eyes.
She is as crisp as untrodden snow.
Her smart frock fits as grass
coats a rolling hill.
Each feature on her face
fine as painted porcelain,
save for her expression.
She stares at me like I might disappear.

"Good morn, with what
may I help you?" I say.

"Where is Ann?" She scrunches up
her nose. She has not removed
her eyes from mine.

"Junior or Senior?" I ask,
and stick two fingers
in the baby's mouth to stop it crying.

The girl be transfixed upon my hair;
she stands at the door still unspeaking.

I repeat, sweet as maple jam,
"Pray, ask you after the little,
or the lady Ann?"

"Margaret, you got away!"
I startle a mite when Ann Junior
calls from behind me, and the baby
lets out a great wail.

Ann says, "Mercy,
this is my cousin, Margaret.
Margaret, this is *Mercy*,
the one I told you of."

Margaret looks to judge me
up and down
with her stone eyes,
but I won't abide it.

I just smile at her, come to play
with a little girl.

A REAL BEAUTY
Margaret Walcott, 17

I click the door
behind me so none
can hear, especially not her.
"She ain't that pretty," I say.
Ann's head nods,
but her eyes do not agree.

And neither does her mouth.
Ann says, "Mercy can read and write.
And she has been a servant
since she was eight. She was schooled
when she was only five.
Mercy helps *me* with my lessons."
Ann offers this to me
like it be flavored sugarcane.

"She'll not make a goodwife
with all that reading and such.
'Tis against the Lord's way."
I flop down on Ann's bed.

"Then why has Father made
me work at my lessons?" Ann says.

I flip through the scattered
parchment on her bed,
pages and pages Ann copied over.
"What be this about?"
I point at the text.

Ann looks bewildered
as though I have poured
a pitcher of water down her back.
"Why, Margaret, know you not
the Lord's Prayer?"

"Course I do.
I was testing ye, Ann."
I pick up the page
and say from memory,
"Our Father, who art in heaven."

Ann relaxes her shoulders and laughs.
"You caught me well there," she says.

I nod, but as soon as she turns her back
I grab the parchment paper
and slip it into the pocket of my new skirt.
Maybe if I look at it enough, I'll figure
how to read it.

Then like I be reading fortunes
I crack open an empty egg
for beautiful Mercy.
I try to stop the smile
from devouring my face.
"Pity Mercy cannot marry
for she be an orphan
with no dowry or name."

"Yes, 'tis horrid."
Ann's eyes dig into mine.
"How would you feel?"

I look down
and shake my head.
"I hope never to know."

WHAT THE WINTER WIND BRINGS
February 1692

Bones chatter, while branches
snap heavy with ice.
Something stronger than fever
quakes and curls
through Village girls.
Their screams and contortions
be of awesome proportion.
'Tis a sight to behold,
distraction from cold.

THURSDAY MEETING

Margaret Walcott, 17

Issac motions and we sneak
behind the meetinghouse.
He whispers against my cheek,
"How fare ye, Margaret Walcott?
Needest thou a kerchief?"
I hold up my arm.
"I need not a kerchief
when I have my sleeve."
His lips do curl up
in a sweet curve of smile.
A shuffle of feet
toward the church and he says,
"We best get back."
But when I turn to leave,
Isaac holds me by the elbow
and anchors me to his side.
His breath is smoke.
His lips on my neck
cause me stumble.
Quickly he does release me.
Isaac tugs at his sleeve
and readjusts his collar;
then paces far ahead.
He walks toward his father, hat-stiff,
as though he and I never did speak.
But he must be trembling too.

ABSENT AND ABSENTMINDED

Ann Putnam Jr., 12

"Neither Abigail nor Betty
   was in meeting. They never
were absent from lecture before.
Why are they not here?"
I look into Margaret's eyes as I talk,
   but it is like I speak to the wind.

"Does Isaac not seem dizzy
   on his feet?" she says.

"Isaac? Isaac who? Margaret,
   hearest thou what I say?
Betty and Abigail, where are the girls?
Do you suppose they have the fever?"
But Margaret just stares without response.

So like snow blown by God's breath,
   I drift over to Mercy.
And Mercy whispers, "Curious
the Minister's daughter and niece
were not in church."

LISTEN
Ann Putnam Jr., 12

Mercy and I press
against the doorframe
to hear our elders speak.
Betty and Abigail are still sick,
and if it isn't fever
it is a disease of the soul,
an evil hand upon them.

Could I be to blame?
Did we girls summon
the Devil's magic
telling those fortunes?
I have to reveal
our little egg trick
to Mercy. "Mercy?"

"Hush," she says.
"I want to hear
what they say."

WORK NEVER ENDS
Mercy Lewis, 17

No sun shines on this rainy morn,
but with Missus off to help
with the weaver's wife's afterbirth
my day should be bright.
Except little Ann shadows me wherever I go.

"What did your mother look like?"
she asks me, her eyes big as biscuits.

God's honest truth is it is hard
to picture my mother's face some days.
"She had eyes green as clover
and could spot trouble
coming half a day away."

"I mean was she pretty like you?"
Ann says. A blush flares across her face.

"Yea, she was handsome.
Our servant Rosaline said her skin
was softer than a babe's
and fairer than the Queen's."

"And she is dead? All your family is dead?"

I nod. "They thought my father's aunt
might be living, but—"
I pause and wonder where I hid that letter.
My eyes feel heavy.
"I don't care to talk of this anymore.
I want to rest now. Pray go see
what your sister is about."

Ann looks like I have
called her a cross name or stomped
her favorite doll.

She tugs my sleeve. "Have you heard
the latest tell about the Minister's
daughter and niece?"

"Are they not ill?" I ask.
Ann shakes her head.
"Father said Betty and Abigail
been having terrible fits,
screeching under the table like wild dogs.
Talking words that none understands.
They contort into eights and levitate
above their sheets such as none
can believe their eyes."
Ann pauses for a breath.
"There be more."

"Do tell," I say, and grasp her hand.

"Father says the girls shout as hobgoblins,
like they were Satan's kin.
And ministers from many miles spread
pray all hours by their bedside,
but to no aid.
Reverend Parris even tried the folk remedies:
parsnip seeds in wine,
a draft of soot with heartshorn,
spirits of castor with oil of amber.
Nothing works, no amount of prayer
and fasting ends their spells."

THE MORE I TELL HER

Ann Putnam Jr., 12

I look up at Mercy.
She drinks in my words,
and they seem to light her
from the inside out.
I want to touch the glow
of her hair. I sit on my hands.

"Father says Reverend Parris
kneeled aside his daughter and niece
and named them possessed.
But this was falsely diagnosed,
for the girls fare too well and right
when not afflicted
to be taken of the Devil."
I fall back onto the bed,
out of my breath.

"There is something more."
Mercy clasps my hand. "Tell me."

I look direct into her eyes.
"Father says
somebody in our village
must be doing
witchcraft."

THE GOOD DOCTOR'S GOOD GIRL
Margaret Walcott, 17

Up on Ipswich Road
a girl *my* age, *not* a servant,
boards with Doctor Griggs.
Uncle Ingersoll says
the girl's so quiet you can hear
snowflakes falling 'pon her cheek.

"Elizabeth," I call
when I pass her on the road
back from Uncle's tavern.
She spins her head,
searching for another with her name.
"Good to meet you," I say.
"I'm Margaret Walcott."

She clutches her parcel to her chest.

"Cold today," I say, and she says nothing.
"How fare ye?" I ask her, but still
Elizabeth gives no response.
Is she mute, be she a simple girl?

I try once more. "Have you heard
what goes on at the Minister's?"

She nods, opens her mouth,
but then covers it with her hand
as if she would be slapped for her speech.

I pull her hand away.
"Pray, be not feared to speak.
I shall be your friend, Elizabeth."

Elizabeth shifts her weight side and side.

I whisper, "There may be witches
in this village. Know ye about the craft?"

"'Tis Satan's work," she says.
Her eyes swell and ignite.
"I knew a witch hanged for her poppets
and spells. For the Bible says,
'Thou shalt not suffer a witch to live.'
Exodus chapter twenty-two, verse eighteen."

"Do tell me, friend, all ye know
and hear," I say.

WHO KNOWS WHAT IS BREWING?

Ann Putnam Jr., 12

Even Margaret of the vacant stare
asks, "Do you know further tell
of the Minister's girls?"

She stretches across my bed
and picks up my comb.
She drags it through her hair
rough enough I fear it might break.

"No," I say, though I perfectly well
know what they have been about
at the Minister's house.

"Well, Abigail and Betty
are all folk can talk about,"
Margaret says, and locks her eyes on me
as though she be wishing to stir my pot
and test what ingredients I hold.

I keep my lid closed.

NEVER TELL OF FORTUNES
Margaret Walcott, 17

Ann grabs her comb from my hands
such that she slices my finger.
I suck up the blood bubbling
at the surface of my skin.
"You don't suppose that folk magic
game of yours what called up that coffin—"

Ann's anger smokes from her nostrils.
She grasps my wrist and whispers,
"'Twas thou who wanted to play fortunes."

I wrest free of her and say,
"Ye taught me to read egg whites."

Ann shakes her head.
"No, cousin. Thou art wrong.
If anyone, 'twas Betty and Abigail."
She hugs me against her chest.
"Promise never to tell
we played that game,
else we might be accused
of witchcraft."

I clutch her little hand and whisper,
"No, never."

WASHING OUR HAIR

Margaret Walcott, 17

The basin steams
and Elizabeth reaches
to dunk her hands in the water.
"You'll scorch yourself!
Use that cup."

I tip my head back.
"Aaagghh!" I holler
when she pours
fire on my scalp.

Elizabeth jumps back,
then lowers her head to say,
"Sorry, Margaret. I only meant to . . .
The Doctor likes hot water.
He says it purifies the skin."

She lathers soap in my locks,
then carefully rinses me clean.
She squeezes off the drips,
rubs in aloe,
and dries me with rags—
much better than our maid.

I smile as Lizzie untangles
my gnarls. It feels like my head
be a loom she's unthreading.

"Your turn," I say,
and Elizabeth looks
as stunned as a frozen bird.
Did she think I invited her over
to wash my hair alone?
I unlace the woolen top
of her dress and dunk her hair
in the soapy water. I tug
my pewter comb
through her curls, but never
does she yelp or moan.
I tie her hair up in frayed blue ribbon.

"Come, we'll draft wool
while we dry our hair by the hearth,"
I say, and look for Step-Mother.
When I be sure the beast be hidden,
I take Lizzie's hand and whisper,
"Isaac Farrar kissed me."

Elizabeth gasps, and her eyes
jump like buttons coming loose.

"You never been kissed?"

She rattles her head back and forth.

"Well, it be like sweetest jam.
And Isaac knew quite well
how to spread it," I say.

Elizabeth coughs to signal
that Step-Mother enters the room.

I wink her my gratitude.

TALK OF THE WITCHES

Mercy Lewis, 17

I sneak Ann into my room.
We crouch down by my bed
and whisper like sisters ear to ear
so not a sound escapes the air.
"Did your father truly see the bruises
appear upon Betty and Abigail?"

"Yes, and the girls called out
Tituba, their slave, saying she did teach them
folk magic. The girls also named
the beggar woman Goody Good.
Tituba and Sarah Good are the witches
who've been tormenting the girls."

"Who be Sarah Good?" I ask.

"Sarah Good says unholy words.
She frightens even the Reverend.
She has been accused before."
Ann smiles.

Wilson barks.
I quiet his mouth with my hand.
"And all did believe them?" I ask.

"All that Betty and Abigail say in fit
is listened to like it comes from the town council."
Ann's eyes double their size.

"It was not like this where I came from before."
I pace my room.
"When the children were bewitched, the preachers
tried always to stop them from fitting."

Ann bends to pet Wilson,
but he pulls back his head
like a riled tortoise.
"Not so with Betty and Abigail.
Father stays at the parsonage late
into the night watching them.
Many church members do.
They have chained Tituba up in jail."

I scratch my head.
"Men listening to the words of girls?
Are you certain, Ann?"

"Yes, 'tis true."

"If only ye could visit the parsonage
and see the girls."

"Oh, but I have seen Abigail
this very day. I saw exactly
how she does twitch and shake.
I know what the witches do to torture her."
Ann twists her torso tight as a rope,
then juts her bones inside out.

Much as I might like to cover my eyes
as Ann cripples her body into a sailor's knot,
my arms hang at my sides.
My mouth droops open.

"They call it Affliction," Ann says.
"All are in awe of it."

A flash of mischief crosses Ann's eyes
as she watches me watching her,
like the torch that smokes
heaven's white edge.

I AM AFFLICTED

Ann Putnam Jr., 12

Someone makes my legs
whip about like sheets in the wind.
Someone curls and bends
my arms behind my neck.
All turns black and cold.
"Who goes there?" I cry.

I scream until the room comes lit,
and then I see witches
the same as the Minister's girls—
Tituba, the Parrises' slave, and Goody Good.
I swear to Father 'tis the witches
who twist my limbs and cause me ache.
I blink my eyes and the witches disappear,
but I saw them stand before me,
felt them pinch my arm,
I know that I did.

INTO THE WOODS
Margaret Walcott, 17

Trees don't talk
so we walk far enough
into the thicket
me shivering under Isaac's cloak
so he can kiss me full
on lips, forehead, eyelids,
earlobes, neck, chest
and lower,
and his hands are branches
and he shakes me loose
until it seems I will be
bare as the winter trees.

But the wind kicks up
and I wake and I smell
pine needles. I am an evergreen
I think. I tell him
I don't shed my leaves,
well, not today,
and he takes my hands
and I become the branch
shaking him loose
amidst the flurries of snow.

WHAT BOYS SAY
Margaret Walcott, 17

Girls play
at who will make us husband,
but not boys.

But Ann overheard her mother say
that when they asked Isaac
who he might take in hand
after he returns from the battles,
he did say if he must, well then,
perhaps, Margaret Walcott.

My pulse be fast as a hound after a hare.
"Do tell it again, but more slow
and with all the senses of it,"
I say to Ann.

Ann rolls her eyes
such that I want to pluck
them from her rag doll head.
"'Tis nothing to have a boy
like you; Mercy makes all men turn stare.
Do you not want to hear
of how the witches
did pinch me
and Father told the magistrates?"
Ann asks.

If once and again I hear tell
of Ann and her witch prick,
I might pinch her my own self.

"I feel not well,
and best go home," I say.
I swaddle up for the cold.
But as soon as I leave
I turn up Ipswich Road
toward the dwelling
of my new friend,
Elizabeth.

ON THE WAY TO ELIZABETH
Margaret Walcott, 17

The snow must haze my eyes.
I stand as ice, feet to bonnet,
froze still. Isaac,
all chest thrust forward,
struts across Ipswich Road.
His arms be stacked with firewood.
I look heavenward
to thank the Lord for this good day.
I pull down my sleeves
and hitch up my skirts to meet him.
Then I see her, with her scurvy smile,
the ugliest sinner in Satan's den!
She right traps my Isaac.
She lifts her crinolines over a puddle
and he follows her,
carries that firewood for her
like *he* were *her* servant.
My Isaac trails after a serving girl,
his eyes upon her
like he might lick the snow
from her boots.
I rub mine eyes,
but still that horrible Mercy.

I pick up skirt and run.

TURN YOUR BACK
Ann Putnam Jr., 12

A wind blows outside the parsonage
and slaps my hair to my face.
"Margaret," I call her name,
but she pretends not to hear.
Margaret thumps over to that new girl,
Elizabeth. And without Betty or Abigail,
the eyes of the town stare on me alone,
the new afflicted girl. I shudder, a single
leaf dangling a barren branch.

"Ann." Mercy's hand rests upon my shoulder.
"How fare ye? Feelest thou any pricks or pinches?"

I shake my head.
Mercy nods and says, "Still, I shall sit
aside you, lest you need aid."

This will be the finest Thursday lecture
I ever did attend.

SECRETS
Margaret Walcott, 17

Elizabeth hesitates.
She fixes on her boots,
battered and mud-splashed.

"Well, take them off and come in," I say.

Her fingers twitch
like the pulse of a bird's neck
as she corks off her shoes.
Her eyes avoid me.

She wears no stockings
and her legs be spotted purple and blue.
"What happened?" I ask.

"I have no stockings and 'tis cold,"
she says quickly, hiding away her feet.

"Keep these couple then. They be old,
but will give thee some warmth."

"Thank ye." Elizabeth smiles.

Sunlight forms a patch 'pon my quilt.
"'Twas my mama's. We sewed it together
from the dress Mama wore on the boat
crossing to here."

"'Tis pretty." Elizabeth begins. "My mother—"

"Lizzie, can you keep a secret?"
I close my bedroom door.
"For I must tell someone, but only one I can trust."

"None shall know what you say to me,"
Elizabeth says, and falls hush.

I let go my breath. "Isaac Farrar,
he says he will marry me,
and I do love him.
But I spied him handling wood for Mercy,
the Putnams' servant girl,
them alone in the forest together,
Isaac smiling at her like he covet her,
and I know not what to do."

Lizzie follows each of my words.
"The Lord will guide you, Margaret.
We must pray for Isaac."
She bows her head.

Two minutes pass
and I can bear no more silence,
no more praying on this.
I pull Lizzie off her knees.
"What hear ye 'bout the third witch accused?"

"Uncle Griggs says Sarah Osborne
be old, mad and bedridden," she says.

"But didst thou know Goody Osborne
lived in sin before marrying her own servant?"

Elizabeth gasps and shakes her head.

"Yea," I say. "And Goody Osborne
tried to cheat Ann's father and his brothers
out of her late husband's trust."

"That be a sin," Lizzie says.

I nod and say,
"And Goody Osborne be a witch."

PRECIOUS
Mercy Lewis, 17

"Ann, dear, pray come out
from behind the drapery,"
Missus Putnam says,
her voice honey spun and soft.

Missus motions for me
to pick up Ann,
no longer a baby.
I cannot breathe
until I set Ann on the divan.

Ann grabs my hand.
Her tremors grow so powerful
that they tumble into me,
and I too jitter and twitch.

Missus says, "Ann, dear,
you will be better.
Father and Uncle Edward
and Mister Hutchinson and Mister Preston
are off to the magistrates.
The Constable will arrest those witches.
Before 'morrow Sarah Good and Sarah Osborne
will be with Tituba in shackles. And, my dear child,
I pray you will terror no longer."

She strokes Ann's hair
as she screeches for me to
"Fetch the child some tea!"

"Yes, ma'am," I say, and turn
toward the kitchen.
The Missus cradles
little Ann in her arms.
And for the first time I can recall
Missus looks at Ann
as though she is something
precious,
dear as her necklace
of gems.

INGERSOLL'S ORDINARY

March 1692

Cider flows inside the tavern,
for Ingersoll's serves
a hearty stew
of witch fever.
All who enter and imbibe
do lick their lips for more.

Sure as meat makes a pie,
the villagers be certain
that Satan is among them.
The brisk spoons of girls
ladle fear
into everyone's bowls.

FIRST TIME IN THE COURTROOM
Ann Putnam Jr., 12

I sit not aside Mercy or Margaret,
but next to Abigail and little Betty.
They drag in Goody Good
for her formal examination.
Shall she remain in jail?
Shall she face trial?
I wish to run from the room.

The others kick and scream.
I kick and scream too,
for I know not what else to do.

All the people packed into the meetinghouse
believe the witches do harm us.
And our elders cannot be wrong.
Certainly the Reverend
and the magistrates
and Father
can tell what be false
and what be the truth.

FLATTERED

Mercy Lewis, 17

Uncle Edward back from the north
with a slanted nose
and a hollow space
instead of a bottom tooth,
he wishes to trap me
like he traps dinner
with one eye down the barrel.
In the day I curve him off my trail,
never to be caught by manners
well and polite, his friendly smile,
his buttons right and tidy.
Most girls would blush and curtsy
and feel flattered as a pretty dress.
I know better.
Living with Reverend Burroughs's
roving hands schooled me well.

Night crawls over the house.
Footsteps creep down the hall
like a low drumbeat.
Two eyes flash against the dark,
husky breath at the doorframe,
a glint of leather boot.
Edward be leaning there.

The scream starts
inside my stomach,
what shall I do?

Fore I can move,
I be sheltered by fur.

Wilson bares his teeth
and threatens to wake the house.
Edward fists his anger,
but he cannot harm
Mister Putnam's favorite dog.
Edward turns his heels
and leaves me with my Wilson.

MOTHER'S ORDERS
Ann Putnam Jr., 12

Mercy nuzzles Wilson
as she sets down his bowl.
Her eyes look bruised and tired.
"Can I help thee?" I start to ask her,
but Mother summons me, "Ann!"

"Follow not our serving girl."
Mother lies still in her bedclothes.
"Bring your lessons in here,"
she commands.
I grind my teeth.
Oh, the day will be long and dull!
I scratch my head.
Perhaps I shall fall prey to the witches.

THE PAIN OF AFFLICTION
Mercy Lewis, 17

The Missus and I
tend Ann by turns.

I grasp Ann's hand
and try to pull her
from her nightmare.

The specter she sees today
she names as Goody Proctor,
wife of the tavern keeper
who sells drink to traveling men
who act like slant-eyed, heavy-tongued dogs
come springtime.
Goody Proctor is known herself
to have cursed her neighbors'
calves and horses
and husbands.

Ann squeezes my arm.
Her hand is almost
as big as my own,
and she is strong
as a fuming bull.
Her fingers are brittle pins.

She clenches my wrist
as though she wants
to lead me somewhere
in her half sleep.
She reaches toward my face.

"It hurts," she yelps.
"Make it stop. Make her stop."
Ann's mouth foams like surf
on a stormy morn. Her face pales.

But her eyes blaze.
They bid me,
Come into the madness, Mercy.

And then I see it,
in the deep black of her eye,
a cavern,
a place
amidst the suffering
it seems
a girl might escape.

A REAL PROBLEM

Margaret Walcott, 17

Her room be bare,
except for the wood cross on her wall.
What kind of girl got nothing,
not even a brush or a porcelain pitcher?

"Elizabeth, Isaac can't like
Mercy over me?"
I twist hair round my finger
and yank a few strands from my head.
"Could be he was just being
helpful carrying that wood?"
I pace round the bed.
"Or could be worse than I suppose!
Lizzie, what'll I do?
He is all I want in this world.
I'll give him many good sons.
I wish the unrighteous on that Mercy!"

I look at Elizabeth, who should
be nodding her head to agree
with me or calming me
with her sweet assureds,
but she just glares forward,
tugging down her sleeve.

I wave my hands before her eyes
and not a blink of her lids.
Her arms twist behind her
slow and tight like roots
of a tangled old tree.
I try to move them back
to place but have not the strength.

I scream, for the pain
crashes over my friend's face
like a tidal wave,
but she cannot make noise;
barely can she make breath.

"Help! Doctor Griggs!
Somebody! Help!
Elizabeth be afflicted!"

Elizabeth's hand nearly
strangles my wrist
as if to shout, "No!"

GROUP OF AFFLICTED

Mercy Lewis, 17

Outside Sunday meeting
Betty and Abigail stand
stationed aside the Reverend.
One arm around each,
he shows them off like they are sons
wounded and home from war.

Doctor Griggs shoves forth Elizabeth.
She joins the Reverend's small troop of seers.
Elizabeth twists down her sleeve,
tottering on her boots as though
she be not sure she belongs.

Missus says, "Ann, step now
and take thy place among them."

Ann stares up at me and I shrug.
I understand why her foot
sticks in the snow.
The other girls hunch
tattered and wan,
unsteady and unready
for all the eyes
which fall upon them.

"Go on, stand ye by the Reverend,
and tell all what thou hast seen."
Mister Putnam's voice disavows
hesitant feet. Ann scurries forth.

Missus looks to join her,
but Thomas Putnam raises his hand
and shakes his head. "Little Ann
will sit aside me in meeting today."
He hands Missus his cloak,
whistles Wilson to his side
and clasps the hand of his daughter.

Missus gasps as though a door
be shut upon her breath.
She tosses Mister's cape to me
without a glance my direction.

Out the corner of my eye
I see Margaret snicker.

Ann stands before the parsonage
held steady by her father,
and all look on her, amazed.

Margaret plods toward the others,
unarmed, without her father at her side.
"Maaaargaret," her step-mother crows
loud as a pestered gull.
"Thou art not a seer."

I be nearly tempted to pity
Margaret when turned eyes
shame her face red.

In the diversion, Ann's panicked
brow raises to me,
as if I should tell her what to do.

I shake my head
as she is swallowed
into the church.

MOTHER TELLS WHAT I SEE

Ann Putnam Jr., 12

"An old woman rocks
in my grandmother's chair,
knitting black baby's stockings.
I know this old woman
but don't remember her name,"
I say quickly to avoid interrogation.

Mother squeezes my hand and doesn't let go.
"Ann, dear." She locks eyes with me.
"Is it Rebecca Nurse who torments you?"
Mother smiles and nods her head. Her eyes swirl.

The name Nurse is not to be whispered
in my house, for that family stole land
from my mother's father before I was born.

I stretch to seek Mercy.
But Mother blocks her from view.
My fingers turn metal cold with pain.

"Yes. Goodwife Nurse.
That is who sits in Grandmother's chair,"
I say. Mother releases my hand.

BEWITCHED
Margaret Walcott, 17

"That bonnet be right smart."

I turn and look,
but none is on the trail,
except a red-chest sparrow
high-stepping his pin legs
in the dirt.

"Margaret."

"Art thou bewitched?"
I point a twig at the feathered one,
and he flies away.

Laughter bubbles like notes out of a flute
and the chuckling can't belong but to one.
"Isaac?" I say his name so quiet
only the leaves know I speak.

He pulls the string under my chin,
and my bonnet falls to the ground.

I feel all the hair sprout
horrid and toadlike from my head.

My one hand quick smooths it down,
the other fastens my cap back in place.
But he undoes it with more speed.
This time I yank the cloth over my ears
and hold tight. With less than a tug
he snatches my bonnet high above my reach.

My face heats. "Pray, let me have it back!"
My fists wish to beat his chest.
Why and how could he
carry that wood for any but me,
not to say a servant,
not to speak for that lowly wench?

"Margaret, what be?" Isaac dabs
one finger under my eye
as it starts to spill its sadness.

"Isaac." His father calls his name
from not twenty paces away.

Isaac hands back my bonnet
and with a fast wave good-bye,
he makes his leave of me.

A NEW WITCH ACCUSED
Ann Putnam Jr., 12

Uncle Edward asks, "Ann, what clothes
doth Goodwife Corey wear when she attacks ye?"

My breath quickens, and I gasp like I be drowning.
I cannot see what clothes Goody Corey wears.

"I cannot see the Invisible World," I say.
"I feel Goody Corey choke and prick me.
She tells me it is her who torments me so.
She says my sight will not return until evening
and then she will pay me off for daring
to name her to you." I collapse under my words.

Uncle and Deacon seem satisfied
with my explanation, satisfied
as one feels after a hearty meal.
The men journey off to Martha Corey.

Only Mercy's eyes contain questions.

HEARSAY
Ann Putnam Jr., 12

Mercy looks up at me as she lifts the baby.
I feel tall. She motions for me
to press my ear against her lips.
"Who is Martha Corey?" she asks.

"Father and Reverend Parris say
Goody Corey speaks against
the existence of witches in our village."

"Ann, dear." Mother stands behind me.
"Whisper not in Mercy's ear.
I can hear plain what you say."
She sits on the ottoman.
"Goody Corey also gave birth to a child
out of wedlock with one of her slaves,
or maybe 'twas just a servant,
but the baby was not only Puritan white."

"So then all believe her to be a witch,"
Mercy says.

"Not all, for Martha Corey be pious
and a church member," Mother says,
and smooths the hair off my forehead.
"But she will be judged a witch."

FIRST SIGHT

Mercy Lewis, 17

Master Putnam tests his daughter
like a cruel schoolmaster.
He walks her tormentor, Martha Corey,
into the house. Ann bends and shrivels,
and when she claims Goody Corey
is the cause, her tongue shoots
from her mouth and her teeth
clench down on it until blood comes.

When I bend to aid her,
Ann whispers to my ear alone,
"Do you not see a man on a spit,
Goody Corey roasting him like a boar?"
She squeezes my hand,
but I yank it away. I feel a pang of pity
for her, but 'tis not my place to bear
her father's investigation.

Ann says, "I see the Invisible World.
There," and she points to the left.
"A man skewered on a stick
turns roasting like a boar.
And Goody Corey turns the spit."

"Come, Mercy." Ann's whisper to my ear
is a plea and a command. "Come with me, now."

I shake my head at Ann.
Hot as the man roasting on the stick
I feel the eyes of the Putnam men
scathe my skin.
I wish for twelve shawls
to burrow beneath,
for my own dress feels ripped apart.

I split and chasm—Ann's voice calls,
"Here, Mercy." She offers me a place
the others cannot touch,
a place I can crawl inside and wear as home.
I blink my eyes. Mister Putnam
and the other men blur to a low hum.

But will any believe the servant girl
sees the Invisible World?

Ann's moaning and writhing envelop me.
I let myself slip into the cavern.
I fathom Goody Corey's specter
strikes me swift with an iron rod.
I fall in pain worse than a whipping,
and gasp, "I see it too! I see it too!"

Ann points at the real Goody Corey.
"Make her go."
Master Putnam sends Goody Corey away.

My limbs twist and shake
even more violently than Ann's,
for I am bigger than she.
It takes three men to hold me down,
though none seem unhappy for the task.

The night cools and howls
near midnight.
But only Wilson dares
close his eyes.
The wooden chair
I rest upon trembles, then rocks
back and forth on its legs.
All believe 'tis the witches
who tremor my chair.
The men study my every movement,
but this staring be reverent.

WHAT IS GOOD,
WHAT IS GREAT
AND WHAT IS AMAZING

Ann Putnam Jr., 12

What is good about witches
is that when I call out "Mother,"
Mother listens and replies,
"Yes, dear Ann."
And when I do say
I see the Invisible World
Father doth bend an ear
and hold me upon his lap.
But what is most amazing
about Affliction
is that Mercy is come along now
as my sister.
She eats beside me at the table.
We sit in meeting and examination as *kin*.

BETROTHED
Margaret Walcott, 17

Isaac and his father shake off their hats
and shake hands with my father
fore they sit at the table
and swallow five mugs of cider
and whisper for two and a half hours.
I crouch down, as my legs
ache from standing and spying.

"Peer not round the corner,
Maaaaargaret." Step-Mother shakes
my shoulders and I nearly wail
like a boat entering harbor.
My heart breaks in fast waves
against my skin.

"You frightened me," I whisper
through grinded teeth.

She thrusts me back
so she can best see.
"Looks as though Isaac will marry you
after all." Step-Mother shrugs.
"Though I cannot know why."

"How do you know we will be wed?"
I ask her.

"Well, there be no brawl and your father
just patted Isaac's back."

I run toward the front room,
but Step-Mother catches my skirt
and winds me back into her
like I be a spool of thread.
"Oh, no. That be affairs of men,"
she says.

"But I just want to rejoice
with Isaac a moment."

"Rejoice," she snorts.
"Go and pray now
you make him happy enough."

I sulk down the hall.
Dear Lord, I pray that Mercy
may find torment so great
she recovers not
and then Isaac shall be happy
with only me.

BECAUSE I CALL HER WITCH

Mercy Lewis, 17

They bind Goody Corey's hands
in front of her
like a mock prayer.
She bows down her head.
The night wind
slices her back in a cross
shoulder to shoulder,
and I hold the blade.
The stain of red is upon my hands.
I point "Witch, witch"—
and they cart her away.
Creaking wheels cut the snow.
Goody Corey's face softens
from its haggard knot
into my mother's freckled cheek.
I fall to knees,
beg, "Forgive me.
I will take the lash and chain,
just set her free."

Wilson licks my fingers,
and I wake.

The sun already half-mast
and yet none calls my name
to fetch or serve,
but they take me now
more like one of their own.
Be this the Lord's way?

OUR PLACE

Mercy Lewis, 17

Inside Ingersoll's ordinary,
the tavern owned by Margaret's uncle
with food and housing for travelers,
my place aside Ann, Elizabeth,
Betty and Abigail awaits me.
Margaret also sits at our table.

All nod "Good day" to us seers
as though we are menfolk,
not maids or children.
Ears perk and lean
toward our table.
The town asks
what have we seen
of the Invisible World?

Elizabeth's eyes a royal purple,
her face filled with scratches
like she wrestled a wild boar.
"Martha Corey did torment me
last night," Elizabeth whispers to us
as though she means it.
Her sleeves stretched over her hands
like mittens.

Margaret yanks Elizabeth to her feet
so all can observe the girl's swollen face.
"Martha Corey did beat Elizabeth,"
Margaret brags to the crowd, and yet
she be the only girl at the table,
still, without the vision
to see.

Margaret brushes my arm
as she takes her seat. She jumps back
as though she might catch pox
should her skin fall on mine.

"What be, Margaret?" I ask her.

She swallows as in disgust.
"How could any believe
the words of a serving girl?"

Ann grabs Margaret's arm.
"You will speak to Mercy with respect
or leave this table, Margaret."

Silence clamps tight the bench.
The other girls pick
at the bread crumbs dusting their plates.

Margaret nods at Ann.
She looks not on me.

Abigail reveals a bruise upon her arm
and announces with the volume of an angry reverend,
"Rebecca Nurse pinched and pricked me."

The crowd gasps. All lose their breath
at the same moment.
"Rebecca Nurse is a Gospel woman,"
someone whispers.

Abigail shakes her arm.
"Aye, but the evidence be right here."

Ann says, "Rebecca Nurse visited me too."
The noise nears rowdy.

Elizabeth huddles us round.
She speaks just above the clamor,
"We are called. The Lord sends us
to find the devils among us.
We must follow only the Lord."
The little girls nod.
I slowly nod too.

But Margaret acts is if she hears nothing,
as though she were as deaf
as the plate before her.
She straightens her dress
and adjusts her bonnet's bow.

THE BITE THAT TURNS YOU
Margaret Walcott, 17

I scan Ingersoll's.
There's only a smattering
of folk in from the rain,
which sounds like fingers
drumming 'pon the roof.

I turn to sally home.
I scream liken the angels
might hear me,
and hold up my wrist.

Visiting Reverend Lawson
and Uncle Ingersoll catch me
fore I hit the earthen floor.
They settle me at a table
and examine my arm.

By candlelight all see
that I been bit.
The Lord adds me
to the group
of those who see.

I am not left behind.
My eyes bloom wide
and pretty as the rest
of the flowers
growing wild
in the witches' garden.

A GARDEN TOGETHER
LAYS ROOT
April 1692

The mayflowers
bloom now.
Heart-shaped pink and white
blossoms sweeten the wind.
Winter's scraggly witch hazel
and furred pussy-willow buds
crouch not alone
on the hillside.
The spring air smells
ripe and ready.

IMPIOUS DISRUPTIONS
Margaret Walcott, 17

Meeting seems smaller near the pulpit.
'Tis like we be closer to the Lord.
The front pew smells not
of dung-covered boots.

Martha Corey grips her bench,
refusing to look on us girls
now she been accused.

Though none dares defy
a preacher during sermon,
Abigail do rise and say
to the visiting Reverend,
"Stand up and name your text."

Ann announces that Goody Corey's
spirit and her yellow bird
perch high above the congregation.
She says the black-eyed bird flies
to Reverend Lawson's hat
hanging on the front door peg.
"I see it too!" Betty says.
Mercy and Elizabeth nod and agree.
Do they all really see except for me?

Abigail cries and points at Goody Corey,
"Witch and her familiar!"
Isaac shakes his head
when she cries out.
His eyes scold and judge.
His face full of disgust
like Abigail speaks
in drunk soldier's tongue.
Reverend Parris and Mister Putnam
hush us then: "Quiet your tongues
and let good Minister Lawson
finish his sermon."

I sneak behind the meetinghouse
before afternoon sermon,
but for the first time
Isaac be not there.
My stomach squeezes
and I trip over a rock.
Why is he not there?
What have I done?
Did he not like what I did
in the forest?
Where is Mercy?

Someone seizes my shoulders.
Martha Corey turns me to her and scolds,
"I will dispel these accusations.
I am a Gospel woman.
I will stand victorious
against you and your mischievous friends."
Her breath steams across my cheek.

But before I can speak one word,
the other girls circle round me
like the Queen's guard
till Martha Corey be gone.
Ann says, "Do not fear, Margaret,
that witch will be known."

I nod at her and the other girls.
Except for Mercy. I stare on her.
Sunlight runs over Mercy
and her golden temptress hair
liken some waterfall of jewels.

Who will protect me
from the witch
among us girls?

DISTRACTED CHILDREN
Mercy Lewis, 17

The courtroom chatters and churns.
Goody Corey raises her eyes at us,
as if to say, "I'll get you girls."

Ann's eyes roll back until
only the whites show,
and someone in the crowd cries,
"Bewitched!"

"We must not believe
all that these distracted children say,"
Martha Corey insists as she stands
for examination. Her eyes twitch
gray as a storm. She smooths her skirt,
then rubs her hands together.

Ann, Abigail, Margaret and Betty
all mimic Martha Corey
with the sharp jerking movement
of a wheel catching in a rut,
then pulling free.

"Stop praying, Elizabeth,"
Ann speaks without moving her lips.
She pulls Elizabeth up from her knees.
"Forget not, Martha Corey beat you too."

"Perhaps I was deceived.
Perhaps we were all deceived.
It is not too late to beg forgiveness."
Elizabeth looks to Margaret.

"I know Goody Corey is a witch, Lizzie.
She pricked me last night."
Margaret reveals red bumps on her back.

Elizabeth nods. She rubs her arm
and curls her hands into her sleeves.

Abigail says, "The Devil whispers
in Goody Corey's ear."

Ann hollers, "I see the turning spit
and a man roasting on it,
just beside Goody Corey."

Abigail speaks again,
a cavern's echo of Ann,
"Goody Corey roasts a man
for the Devil."

Margaret and I are to suffer next.
We feel jabbed and strangled
and collapse to the floor.
Margaret kicks her boot
a little too close to my head.

Through clenched teeth I tell her,
"Mind yourself."

Margaret points at Goody Corey,
but it is me she names sinner
with her eyes as she screams out the word.
"Any woman who bears babies
out of wedlock must be a witch."

They bind Goody Corey's hands
with sailing rope. Still,
she flutters her fingers.
Each time she does, our fingers wrench,
shot up by her Devil's lightning.

I stare at my hands,
fingers hooked in pain,
and see something new.
These hands are not just
implements to serve.
They are weapons.

The gavel smashes down.
Goody Corey,
like all other witches
the girls and *I* name,
shall face trial.

CAN WE SEE GOOD?

Mercy Lewis, 17

"I told them witches
I will not eat. I will not
drink. It is blood. It is not
the Bread of Life.
It comes not from Christ.
And I spat at Goody Proctor,
the wife of the tavern keeper,
the one selling whiskey blood."
I pant, uncertain whether I can continue.

Mister Putnam strokes my hand
as though I am his child and says,
"Do tell us, Mercy, what next ye saw."

"A shining figure comes
and all the witches fled.
All I could see was a glorious light,
and the voices of Christ
singing like crystal bells
and telling me I am worthy
to take the book, the Book of Life
from Christ. And then the angels,
all of them in rows singing psalms,
and I pled, 'Please let me stay here,
let me not leave.' But then I woke."

Ann says, "Mercy is chosen.
She's been shown good, not evil,
in the Invisible World.
She is the first to see it."

But Missus Putnam is quick
to shake her head,
"No, Ann dear, others
have seen a man in white."

Mister Putnam hovers near my cheek.
He kisses my forehead.
"Mercy, Satan doth love to present
himself as an Angel of Light.
Good that you did not sign that book.
It were Satan in disguise."

The tears come fast
as a mudslide down my cheeks.
We must see evil.

But then the man I serve
kneels to me,
comforts *me*
with his kerchief.
What shall I do?

POWER BEYOND THE PULPIT
Mercy Lewis, 17

The meetinghouse during lecture
might well be the courthouse.
All of us girls sit in the front pew
like we are the town council,
the heads of family, like we are
disciples of his Grace.

The Reverend blasts,
"Have I not chosen you twelve?"
He looks past us girls and declares,
"And one of you is the Devil."

Whispers whirl around the room.
Eyeballs wander like seeds in wind.
Who is the Devil among us,
the one who betrays?
Which of the good folk
is really a witch?

And then the eyeballs settle,
how water smooths after storm.
The eyes look not
to the preacher to answer
their questions, to guide them,
but to us girls, the Afflicted.

We are the ones who see witches.
The good folk nearly plead,
"Pray tell us who be the witches,
who are the devils in our midst?"

PRAY
Margaret Walcott, 17

Isaac gone before
I might turn to look.
The meetinghouse drains
of members, except for Elizabeth,
who kneels on the hard floor,
her head bowed down.

"Oh, Margaret, fall to your knees
and pray with me."
She grasps my hand
and drags me to the ground.
"Dear Lord, guide our spectral sight.
We follow your call
and bow humbly before you."
Elizabeth's eyes pulse
and her body quivers.

"They wait for us outside."
I tug her arm now.
I do not want Mercy Lewis
broken from my sight
such that Mercy might make
her eyes fall 'pon Isaac,
or worse, his eyes fall 'pon her.

I kneel and whisper in Elizabeth's ear.
"I see you be cleversome,
but pray let us do this not today."

Elizabeth just stares forward
as in a trance. She lies down
'pon the floor with her hands
laced in worship above her head.
"O Lord, lead me in your ways."
She stops all moving
and seems not to breathe.
Be she truly tormented by a witch?

The Reverend stalks above us.
"Has a specter hold of Elizabeth?"
he asks me.

I nod yes.

But then Elizabeth pops up,
as if she's possessed, and shakes her head.
"There are no specters here.
We pray to the Lord for guidance."

How dare she defy me?
She must be ill. I clench her arm
tighter than I did intend.

Lizzie tugs down her sleeve.

"Or perhaps Margaret did see a specter," Elizabeth says, and lowers her eyes.

THERE IS ANOTHER: WHAT TO DO WITH THE PROCTORS' MAID?

Mercy Lewis, 17

Not everything in a garden
belongs.
Ruth Warren,
the Proctors' maid,
starts crying witch,
naming the same
witches we do see.
She follows Ann
around after meeting,
inquires about joining
us later at Ingersoll's.
Ann asks if we should
fold Ruth into the blanket
of our group.

I scratch my head.
"What know you of Ruth Warren?"

"She be maid to John
and Rebecca Proctor.
And my father and John Proctor
stand on different sides
of the church aisle."

I advise, "Let us not invite
her into the group yet,
but test her loyalty.
We have been given
a power here together,
we best retain—
to do so we must be strong
and we must be stable.
Nothing foul among us."

LEADERSHIP

Ann Putnam Jr., 12

Mercy and I agree—
in order for us to be stable
someone must take up the head,
must direct the troop through battle,
one of us hold the torch
and shout out command,
else we shall see things unlike
and our voice be scattered,
the body that makes us strong
cut into many pieces.
Betty too young, Abigail too eager,
Elizabeth wavers like a loose tooth,
and Margaret without rank and stature
and breeding and brain—
It must be me.
I am the rightful leader.

ANNOYANCE

Ann Putnam Jr., 12

"They sent Betty away."
Abigail heaves and snorts as she speaks.
She wedges next to me, so I squeeze
into the back of the bench.
I search for Mercy, who was to meet me
at Ingersoll's an hour ago.
"Reverend now depends on me alone
to tell him of the Invisible World.
I seen witches all last night. Goody Proctor
and Goody Nurse and Goody Good."

"Abigail." I wish to fasten my hand
over her mouth. "Tell not our elders
what you see without first speaking to me."

"But Reverend wants me to—"

I cut her words. "Speak not.
Do ye understand me?"

She nods. At this moment,
the sight of Abigail, the scratch of her voice,
brings my lunch to my throat.
Where be Mercy?

"I must go," I say.

"Oh, me too. I'll come with thee,"
Abigail chirps.

I hurry toward the door.

"What have ye seen?" Goodman Rhea
asks as I make to leave the tavern.

"Goody Proctor did bite and pinch me."
Abigail thrusts forth her arm.

"Let us see."
Goodman Rhea bars my exit.

I wish to box Abigail in the cheek:
again she acts without my instruction.

If only Reverend Parris had sent away
both his daughter *and* his niece.

AN INNOCENT RIDE

Mercy Lewis, 17

A young man with shoulders broad as a lake
trails Mister Putnam round the stables.
"Fine mare," he says, his voice
deep earth brown.

"She'll produce fine foal, I believe.
I'll not be trading her if that be
what ye desire, Isaac Farrar."
Mister shakes his head.

"No, sir," Isaac says.
"But might I take her for a ride?"

Mister nods, and Isaac mounts
the spotted mare.
As he grabs hold the reins
his eyes saddle upon me.
I shade red to be caught watching him
for I never do care to observe anyone,
and I ought be slopping the pigs.

Mister Putnam notes my presence with a smile
and calls, "Mercy, come yonder
and fetch a cup of water."

I hand Mister Putnam the tin,
and he squeezes his arm around me.
"Mercy doth see the Invisible World.
She and my daughter Ann,
the Lord has called them."
Mister ruffles Wilson's head,
but calls not his dog away from me.

Isaac fixes upon me
without cessation or flinch.
"I be acquainted with Mercy," he says.

"Beg your pardon, but I do not recall—"

"Do you ride?" he asks like a gunshot,
before I can finish my speech.

Mister twists his face, such that I cannot
tell if it be in anger or pleasure.

"'Tis not proper for a servant—" I begin.

"Do you ride?" Isaac insists, and leads
his own horse over to me.

"Yes, I ride," I say, and hold fast
the reins of Isaac's gaze. I remember
him now—he helped me carry my firewood.
I nearly wish to smile at him, but I cannot say why.

"She cannot ride." Mister grinds his teeth.
"She might find fit and fall.
  It be too dangerous. It be not proper."

Mister turns me round and pushes
me toward the house.

I hear him say to Isaac,
"I think it best if I rest
Beatrice this afternoon.
She was rode hard this morning.
And she does not take well
to strangers."

THE PROCTORS' MAID
RECANTS HER AFFLICTION
Margaret Walcott, 17

    The note Ruth Warren
    nails to the meetinghouse door
    Ann reads to us:

"Thank ye in public
for my condition did but improve.
I do rightly believe the Devil deceived,
and we girls did but speak falsely.
The magistrates might as well
listen to someone insane
and believe what she said
as any of the afflicted persons,
for I submit there be as much truth in madness
as in any of the girls' claims.
Our fits and pains may be put to end
by the Lord's will and concentration of mind.
I humbly ask ye all to forgive
my weakness against the Devil.
Your gracious servant, Ruth Warren."

    "I've a mind to whip
    that Ruth Warren
    same as Goodman Proctor did," I say.

Ann flicks my arm.
"Quiet your tongue.
Cause not disturbance, Margaret."

I want to say, Or else what?
What'll ye do? Who crowned
thee queen? But I hold in
them words for now.

"Do you suppose Ruth be beat
into writing all that?"
I whisper to Elizabeth.

Inside the meetinghouse
all the eyes of the church
lock on us Afflicted
tighter than a bridle.

The question whirling
o'er the rafters, gathering
fast as storm clouds—
If Ruth Warren
recants that she was tormented,
if she can stop her fits,
why then do we other girls
not quit ours?

I stare straight at the pulpit,
try not to let the fire
of their eyes burn my cheeks.

I glance over at Isaac,
want to wave up my hand
and have him lead me out of
this stomach-churning church.
But he never looks my way.

After meeting the sky's
still and gray as a dead fish.
We girls gather in a cluster.

Uncle Thomas speaks loud, so many hear,
"I believe Ruth Warren must have signed
or at least placed her hand upon the Devil's book."
The crowd gasps and nods.

Doctor Griggs adds, "Were our girls
to do that, their aches would leave them too."

"But their souls be blackened."
Reverend Parris's voice shakes the trees.

Abigail steps in the center
of the churchyard
and wilts onto the ground,
falling like a leaf blown down
in a rustle of wind,
her face red as the Devil's book.

"What be she doing?" I say
to the other girls. Ann's eyes boil.

Reverend Parris clasps his scaly hand
on my shoulder. "Be you brave, Margaret Walcott?"
He looks at Mercy and Ann and Elizabeth and me.
"Do not sign that book of blood.
Push away Satan's quill."

We all nod our heads.

Reverend tears down
the note Ruth Warren tacked
to the meetinghouse door.
He rips down her recant
of seeing witches,
her attempt to cast
the rest of us liars.

Soon as he be gone
my step-cousin says,
"Five of us. One of her.
Ruth Warren will face regret."

BAG OF WOOL

Mercy Lewis, 17

All look on Abigail,
fainting skirts upon the ground,
but one.
I feel him once again
wrap gaze around my shoulders
like a shawl, a woolen cloak I need not
on this steam-hot day.
I turn my back to Isaac
though I wish to turn round.

Ann pulls me aside.
"Mercy." She sounds
as though she holds stones
on her tongue. "Ruth Warren,
how shall we make her pay her trouble?"

I whisper to Ann,
"Does any yet look on us?"

"None." Ann taps her foot
as though she has somewhere else to be.

When I draw up my eyes,
his look is still roped upon our group.
I point Ann with my glancing,
"But what of that one with your uncle?"

"None stands by Uncle and Father,
save Isaac Farrar, Margaret's betrothed,"
Ann says. "And he always be staring this way."

"Your cousin will be wed?"
I choke out the words.

Ann nods, then insists,
"What of Ruth Warren?"

"Call her a witch," I say.

BEWARE
May 1692

Ruffle the goose
and she'll snap at your tail,
kick you to stream
and bar you
from the row of ducks.

The water muddies.
'Tis hard to know
where next
to dunk your head
and bite the new fish
when you be
scouting the sea
alone.

UNEXPECTED EXPECTATION
Margaret Walcott, 17

I be weeding the garden
and mending the fence round it
to keep the vermin out
when a large shadow falls
over the seedlings.
Isaac bends to my ear.
"Follow me, fair Margaret."

I can't protest, for as I stand
he be already to the stream
beyond our house.
The sun squints my eyes.
I wipe my hands 'pon my apron
and dash into the woods
past the barn till I find
my sweet one lying in the clearing
flooded in sparkling light
looking more handsome
than Christ himself.
He pats the ground, says,
"'Tis a fine day."

I nod and lie beside him.
He curves me against him
like a belt drawn into a loop.

His kisses tender but brutal,
I wish them never to end.
He begins then at unlacing
my dress. I shake my head.

"But we are betrothed," he says,
and slides a hand beneath
my petticoat.

I feel cold with fright
as though the day be winter ice.
I skirt away from him.
"I think I hear Father call me," I say.

Isaac's eyes roll
and he blows out
an angry sigh
as he places my hand
in that same unholy place
beneath his clothes
he did afore in the woods.
"Not all be as cloistered
in their stockings as thou," he says.

I pretend not to know
what he does imply,
close my eyes
and set to work
while whirling high above us
the wind screams
wild lashings
across the leaves.

THREE SISTERS

Mercy Lewis, 17

The breeze smart
against my neck,
dewy leaves and grass
tickle my nose.
Wilson and I wander
a new route
this morning
on the way to Ingersoll's.

Across the field
out in their garden
they praise the day
like three smiling
blossoms.
Rebecca Nurse
and her two sisters
plant and weed.
Laughter sprinkles
across the soil
as Charlotte slips
in the mud.
Rebecca
lifts Charlotte to a stand,
brushes off her skirt.

I wish to rush across
the meadow
offer my hand,
and join the row of happy sisters.

I stare at my hands,
my horrible filthy hands,
and run.

ANN DECIDES

Mercy Lewis, 17

She knows her little fists
like cannonballs
have the power to crumble
fortress and family.
She decides that Goodwife Cloyse,
the sister of Rebecca Nurse,
will be next accused.
"Sister of a witch.
She must also be a witch,"
Ann says.

Abigail's words jump from her mouth
so she be the first to say,
"Goodwife Cloyse did flee meeting
last Sunday right in the middle,
and she has not been back to the parsonage."

Margaret nods. "And she has been speaking out
against the accusation of her sister."

Ann looks to me to add comment,
but I just stroke Wilson's head.

"But I never did see the specter
of Goodwife Cloyse.
Did ye all?"
Elizabeth's voice be quiet,
but her words be loud.

Margaret clasps Elizabeth's hand.
She says the words that Ann
wishes would come from my lips.
"This matters not.
Kin what stand up for each other,
must make their home in jail."

Elizabeth rises to leave our table.
Her uncle enters the ordinary
and she quickly sits down.
Her body trembles
as she tugs upon her sleeves.

KEEP QUIET

Ann Putnam Jr., 12

Just before sun's at mid-sky,
the meetinghouse stacks with people.
I grab Abigail outside the courtroom.
"You best keep quiet sometimes.
You cannot see everything."

Goody Cloyse stands first in the confession box.

Abigail says, "I saw Goody Cloyse
and Goody Nurse serve our blood
at a meeting of the Devil's
where forty witches come to my uncle's pasture,
congregating till a fine man in white
scared them away."

When Goody Cloyse faints
and the crowd's eyes are diverted,
I kick Abigail hard enough she squeals.

A second witch appears chained before us.
When the magistrate asks,
"Does Goody Proctor hurt you?"
Mercy and Elizabeth and I cannot form words.

Abigail opens her mouth wide as a baby bird.
I stuff it with my bonnet.

The rest of us flap like geese in a pattern.
I head the formation,
and our wings fly all the same speed.
We girls shake together
whenever a witch looks our way.
And the witches become felled birds
the constables chain and cage in jail.

QUESTIONING OUR POWER
Mercy Lewis, 17

I scan around the tavern
and could pinch myself
that we girls should sit here
nearly daily now,
but as the witches pinch us first
and so many folk
be ripe to believe,
I try to accept my seat.

Across the street
some whose family
stand in the confession box
or those who never did like
the selection of Reverend Parris
as village minister,
they eye us girls
with tar and gravel
as though we ought
be the ones chained
to the jailer's wagon.

Abigail rattles her mouth,
the excited babe showing
off how she has learned to speak.
"I saw the specter of Reverend Burroughs,

one who was pastor before
in Salem Village, leading
a group of witches outside
the parsonage last night."

How names she my old master?
How knows she what a true wizard he was?

Margaret laughs. "You cannot know
'twas Minister Burroughs."

"Reverend told me it was so,"
Abigail nearly shouts. "He said
that Reverend Burroughs was acting
the Grand Conjurer, the leader of the witches."

"What matters what your uncle says?"
Ann thrusts Abigail into the back of the bench.
"I am the one to say!"
A grand hush ripples across the tavern,
and all the folk stare on us.

Even Ann quiets then.
She nods at me. "Come, Mercy,
we best be heading home.
All of you best go home and pray."

PROBLEM CHILD
Mercy Lewis, 17

"I just sit there and stitch
while Abigail screams and runs
about the room till they carry her out,
and it is always like this with her,"
Margaret says, and narrows
her eyes in a sneer.

"Why does she not listen to me?"
Ann shakes her head.

Under our table at Ingersoll's
Wilson snuggles beside me
without so much as a yap.
Margaret's feet stack one upon the other
in a tangle. Her skirt sticks under her rump
in a ball like she's a little beggar girl.
How can one so uncouth be betrothed?

"What are you looking at?"
Margaret asks me.

"Nothing," I say.

"Pay attention," Margaret says.
Her voice slaps my hand.
"We've a problem with Abigail."

Ann says, "Something must be done.
Nothing foul must be among us."

My feet go cold like I've slipped
into winter's pond without boots.
Why did Ann not discuss this with me?

Margaret flicks her hair behind her shoulder.
"Ignore her. Act as she does not exist."
She knocks over a mug of ale.
I turn from the smell.

"But Abigail knows not what she does,"
Elizabeth says as she mops the table
with her apron.

The threat in Ann's stare
could frighten a wolf.
"Elizabeth, you are *wrong!*"

Elizabeth shrinks back.

Ann then softens her tone.
"I fear if we teach not Abigail
a lesson, she shall place
her hand upon Satan's book
as Ruth Warren hath done."

Ann stands up, makes herself
the height the rest of us are
when seated. She declares,
"Abigail is as one laid to grave.
Speak to her no more."
Not another word to be said.

RANDOM
Incantation of the Girls

Sour voices on the wind
name us liars, say we sin.
Listen not
to girls but men.

For the witches we do name
pass their days in public shame
or come from families
Putnams blame.

So if we girls shall keep our place
we'll see some witches none can trace,
folk we've never
seen of face.

OUTCAST

Ann Putnam Jr., 12

Abigail's sightings mismatch
ours like sleeves cut
from different fabric.

Margaret, Mercy, Elizabeth and me
call new witches into court,
the first of whom we have never seen,
Bridget Bishop of Salem Town,
the woman they say bewitches
children to death.
We also name Giles Corey
and his gruesome acts,
the old man who,
before any of us we were born to see it,
beat his servant to his last breath.

But Abigail sees neither
Goody Bishop nor Goodman Corey.
She can no longer sit beside us
on the testimonial bench.
The villagers see her not.
She be as a ghost to them.
For I have made her invisible.

A WITCH I HAD NEVER SEEN BEFORE

Ann Putnam Jr., 12

"I know her to be Deliverance Hobbs."
I point my finger at the old witch
in the dark green cloak
who none of the other girls
know by face.
I only know the witch
called to question
because Mother pointed her out to me
before she sat me down upon my bench.

We rattle and roll upon
the floor, but our sounds do not echo
through the room. I must thrust
five pins through my hand
beneath my skirt before
the courtroom screams, "Witch!"

Deliverance Hobbs confesses
with her hands tied upon the stand.
She unpeels her skin
during Judge Hathorne's examination
and admits that witch blood
courses her veins.

"What do we do now?" I ask Mercy.

"When a witch confesses,
we stop our fuss," she says
as Mercy's wails bury their sound
and her body falls motionless
as a dead cat.

The courtroom hisses
as they drag away Deliverance Hobbs.
Mercy tugs my arm and says,
"Good that she confessed.
One less voice weakened
our screaming.
There was power in five."

SILENT TREATMENT AT OUR TAVERN TABLE

Mercy Lewis, 17

"Ann," Abigail hollers,
   but Ann has iron in her ears.
   She will not even turn toward Abigail.

Abigail stands before Elizabeth,
   looks up to her with prayerful eyes.
   "What be happening?" Abigail asks.
   Elizabeth coils her hands into her sleeves.
   She stares through Abigail
   as though she were air.

"Margaret, please," she begs.

Margaret stands
   and Abigail blocks her way.
   A hard shoulder
   into Abigail's nose and cheek,
   and Abigail skids to the floor.
   Margaret tramples over
   Abigail's crumpled body
   without even a glance down.

The tears fire across Abigail's cheeks.
   She swipes them away.

"Is this punishment for what I see?
For what I tell? For my talk
of Minister Burroughs
and his commune of witches
grazing in our pasture
with their black hoods and red books
and drinking of Satan's blood?"

Abigail now looks on me.
I wish to set her free, but
she kneels down before Ann.
"I am sorry. Pray do tell me
what to say, what to do,
and I promise to do
as you command," Abigail says.

Ann pats Abigail's head
like she rubs the pup
at her feet, tousles Abigail's hair
and pinches her cheek.
She looks at the rest of us
and then points at Abigail
crouched upon the ground.
"Stay, girl," she says.
"Do exactly as I say
and I might let you
remain with us."
And Abigail does.

THE GRAND CONJURER

Mercy Lewis, 17

My vision of the Devil
be that crooked-teeth grin
of the man who took me in,
the one who they say can lift
six-foot muskets with his little finger.
He who holds up his book
to timber little girls with one blow.
His red, hot hands
roamed my arms
and inside my discomforts
like a pinching burn.
I found nowhere to run
and nobody to call for help
when he called himself
Reverend and master
and father of the house
and I be but an orphan
of eight.

"What witches, wizards and specters
have you seen in the Invisible World, Mercy?"
They ask me again today.

And I think perhaps
I can recall one bad dream
I had of a Grand Conjurer
last night.

WHAT I DO FOR MERCY

Ann Putnam Jr., 12

Night crawls across the sky,
and a trumpet screams
from the pasture beside the parsonage.
I twirl around, but no one's there.

I say to Father,
"I rub my eyes and appears,
same as Mercy saw last night,
a meeting of witches in the clearing
gathered on their poles,
drinking Devil's blood,
and Reverend Burroughs
stands at the head.

He lectures the witches,
'We will claim New England.
Begin in Essex County
and overtake Salem Village.
One battle, one witch at a time,
until all the land be ours.'"

My father nods agreement.
"Reverend Burroughs be
the Village pastor before ye were born.
He is a thief and a liar.

Of course, he be a witch."
Father straightens his hat
and sets off to visit
the magistrates again.

FEELING QUITE RED
Margaret Walcott, 17

He come in the tavern sweaty
from a day in field and barn.
I wish hard that Isaac will
trot over to me and demand
I fetch him a cider,
but he pretends as though
he sees me not, and grabs a bench
aside his mates William and Ben.

I wave my pinkie at him,
but Isaac must weary of me,
as if I be but a fence he must mend
or a heavy log to haul across the bay.
So I anchor beside Ann.
I whisper, "What of Isaac?"

"We've matters to discuss."
Ann angers that I even mention Isaac's name.
She looks to raise her hand to me.

And then do my skirts flame.
I must stand to let the heat
out from under me.
"Can we talk of nothing but witches?
Ye all be mad with this," I say.

Mercy says, "Go on, Margaret,
ye need not remain with us.
Sit with Isaac. Be with thy *betrothed*."
Her eyes shift like shadows of the night.

I inch over to Isaac timid-footed
and tap his shoulder. He swats my arm
away like I be a pesky gnat.
"Do not attend me
when I be among my mates,"
he says quickly.

I look over at the other girls
staring 'pon us.
I smile all my teeth
like Isaac did proclaim
I be the prettiest fowl in the coop.

I hurry toward the door.
Red splotches before my eyes.

REQUEST
Margaret Walcott, 17

"She be all the time foul,"
Step-Mother says to Father.

I creak open the door,
and the room hums with silence.

"Margaret." Father guides me
to a chair. "Your uncle Thomas
has asked that you come to aid
in his home. And I did say you would."

"But I be not a servant."
The tears I been holding
shower 'pon my face.

"Of course not," he pats my head.
"We think there may be more power
in having three seers under one roof.
Perhaps the witches will stop
their torment. Now ready yourself."

I know he be wrong, we will torment
all the more, but I rise to pack my bags.

Father smiles. "Ann's mother
requested that you come."

The corners of my mouth round up.
My aunt Ann—might she
offer some aid with Isaac,
and Ann's mistreatment of me,
and dread Mercy? My feet tingle.
"Yes, sir," I say.

I do not bid Step-Mother farewell.
I just kiss Father's cheek
and slide out the door.

HE IS NOT THE MAN
Mercy Lewis, 17

The tailor of cloths and hides
gazes at me.
I do not know this man
to point a finger at.
Only Ann does that.

"He is upon the beam,"
Ann says, and all look
up to the rafters,
but I see neither person
nor specter there.

Judge Corwin points at the tailor.
"Be this man a witch?"
he asks us Afflicted.

Elizabeth says, "Yes, sir.
He is the one who hurts me."
But her voice quivers
as she speaks, like a branch
rattled in the wind.

Allowed back in court for the first time,
Abigail looks to Ann,
but Ann stares toward the window.

In a voice unsteady
as a one-legged man Abigail says,
"He is the man. He is very like the man."

Margaret says, "Yes, he is very like the man."

The tailor's eyes plead with me.
I shift on the court bench.
"He is not the man," I say.

Gasps and chatter fly
about the court like roused hornets.
Judge Corwin calls, "Silence."

Ann's eyes enlarge
and she demands of Nehemiah Abbott,
the tailor, "Be you the man?"

Ann spits and sputters,
writhes and kicks herself
onto the floor.
She cries, "Did you put a mist on my eyes?"

We are dragged outside
and asked again
to look upon the countenance
of Goodman Abbott.
All the girls nod with me this time.

Though Goodman Abbott
be like the specter,
he is not the same man.

They release Nehemiah Abbott
from his chains.

Little Ann folds her arms,
grinds her toe
into the dusty path.

I stroke her head
and she straightens up.
Her eyes hold back water.
"Did I do wrong?" she asks me.

"Of course not," I say.
"In fact, you did exactly right."

I lift my head
to be for once
not only a part
of the beloved choir
but its lead soloist,
the whole town listening.

LIVING AT THE PUTNAMS'
Margaret Walcott, 17

I fold my skirts into Ann's bureau,
my entire wardrobe crammed
into one drawer.
This room smells like a waste bowl.
I light a taper.

I open the bureau
and Mercy's green shawl lies
inside right where my blue
one ought to go. I toss hers to the floor.

"How dare she go against you
like that? Ye are our leader."
I feel the anger break
through my veins like waves.

"But Mercy was right," Ann says.

I roll my eyes. I turn round
to shake out my blanket,
and Mercy looms in the doorway.
"How long you been loitering there?"
I ask her.

"Long enough." She strokes Ann's arm.
"Ann, would you bring us tea?
I set the water to boiling."

Ann's off like a ship in high gales.
"Now heed me," Mercy says.
As she speaks I spot a flaw of hers—
her teeth are too big for her mouth.

I pull back my arm and crack
my blanket at her face like a whip.
The shock stuns her.
I laugh at her popped eyes
and her hair stuck up
like some frightened cat's.

I strike her again.
She catches the blanket
and drags me toward her.
I dig in and yank backward,
then release my hold,
and she crashes into the wall.

But I let her go with such strength
I tumble myself down too
and bruise my tailbone
direct on the floor.

Mercy smiles and laughs
like we be sharing a joke,
but I do spit 'pon the ground
rather than smile at her.

"Listen, Margaret," she says.

"I'll not listen to thee.
Go and fetch, servant girl."

Mercy slows her voice.
"You best apologize.
You should not treat me as such,
Margaret Walcott. I be offering
you a hand in friendship."

Now I could nearly laugh.
"You are not my friend."

"No," Mercy says,
and she dusts her skirts.
"I suppose I am not."

MARGARET IN THE HOUSE

Mercy Lewis, 17

I pull open another drawer
and not a bloomer to be found.
"Wilson, do the witches
now steal my wash and stockings?"
My sweet dog taps his tail
upon the boards; his tongue
quivers in the affirmative.

Margaret's laughter stokes
the hallways and shatters the ears,
sounding like a spoon scraping an empty pot.
Her cackles are followed by
a deep moan, and Missus Putnam hollers,
"Mercy, fetch a pail and cloth!
Our guest has fallen to fit!"
I wiggle back into my dirty dress
and haul a bucket toward Ann's room,
but halfway there my knees bend under
and I slip to the floor.
I slither as a beast upon the ground
until Mister Putnam carries me
back to my bed.

"The girl is not well.
She cannot attend to others,"

I hear Mister say
after I have been
tucked into my covers
and relieved of my day.

Wilson snuggles aside me.
I stretch my arms above my head,
rise and tiptoe to my window
to watch the morning bowl of sun
soak the fields with God's first light.

"Mercy?"
Ann knocks upon, then opens,
my door.
She holds her brush in hand.
"I cannot be in that room
with Margaret one moment more."

Ann hoists up on my bed
and motions for me to sit up
so she can brush out my hair
while standing on the bed above me.

Ann grumps, "Margaret lights tapers
so my room smells
of wax and burn. I hate it!
Why did she have to come?"

I shrug. "I think she was made to."

Ann throws down her brush.
"I might have to sleep in here with you."

"That would not please your mother."

"My mother will have to learn
to do as I wish, or perhaps
I shall call her a witch?"
Ann's voice is more question
than statement.

"No, Ann, you must never do that,"
I say, and fold her into a seated position.
I give her back the brush
and begin her hand stroking my hair.
But perhaps, you call Margaret . . .
I shake the idea away.

ADVICE

Margaret Walcott, 17

Aunt Ann squeezes my hand.
"A goodwife does always
as her husband does bid her.
To honor him be never a sin."

But what of the betrothed? I want to ask.
Instead I stammer, "What of Mercy?"

"Mercy shall never be a goodwife,
because she is too low
to marry into a proper name.
Her slim beauty will be scoured away
unlike your fair silken own."
Aunt lowers her voice to whispering
and purses her lips like she suffers
from a bitter yam.
"If she be seen at all, 'twill be
as one of tawdry repute."

The tears crash down my cheeks.
How then could Isaac . . . ?
Aunt stares on me till I say,
"I miss Isaac."

"I shall have Thomas ask
Isaac and his father to supper.
What else, child?"

"Ann sees so many *witches*,"
I blurt faster than I did wish.
"I be meaning, I feel as I cannot say
all the specters I see.
I know not the names."

Aunt Ann smiles larger than her land.
"I can help thee. Just speak with me,
dear Margaret, and I will provide thee
names for the specters you know not."
She cradles me to her breast.
"Oh, I am so glad you are come."

SUPPER GUESTS
Mercy Lewis, 17

Mister Putnam straightens his back.
Goodman Farrar, Isaac's father,
a small man with a fair face
and the manners of a minister's wife,
sits aside Mister Putnam.
He nods at Missus Putnam.
"Thank ye for the fine meal."

Missus cooked not a crumb on the table.
"Thou art quite welcome, dear sir," she says.

The baby wails from the nursery.
All mugs beg filling.
And the plates ought be cleared.
I rise to tend the child.
Isaac and his father stand when I do
as though I am the lady
I was born to be.
Margaret clenches her fork.

Ann follows me, and Missus
nearly slaps her back to seating.
"Let Mercy attend to matters alone."
Only Wilson be permitted to trail me now.

I tramp down the hall
and lean over the baby's cradle.
"Shhhh," I say until his storming settles.
I clear the plates, refresh the mugs
and set to wash the pots.

"Mercy," Isaac says from a foot behind me.
"Thomas asks that you sit
and take cider and tea with the family."
Even though he just supped,
Isaac looks at me as though
he has not eaten in weeks
and would lick
my palms to taste me,
I smell to him so sweet.

Wilson begins a growl,
but I muzzle his snout.

How lovely would it be to witness
Margaret the Mean, the bloomer thief, churn
because of my doings for once?
I flick my curls behind my shoulder
and bloom my eyes as petals
at Margaret's beau.
I drop the cloth in my hands.
Isaac bends to pick it up,
and I stoop too.

Isaac breathes upon my neck.
"Ye are—" he begins.

"Your father calls you!"
Margaret's voice severs our air.
But Isaac does not cut his stare from me.
Margaret quivers in her speech.
"I shall stay and help Mercy."

I scrub the pan to rid it
of grease and burn.

Margaret clamps my arm.
"Do not speak to him," she threatens.

"I did not," I say.

I wipe my hands, turn from her
and swirl into my place
aside Mister Putnam.
Isaac's eyes fasten on me
tighter than the collar at my neck.

Margaret ruptures in fit.
"Goody Hobbs pinches me!"

Isaac greens. He shakes his head.
His father, who has offered

not an impolite word the night long,
says, "We shall be off,"
and leaves without finishing his tea,
without a "thank you" or "good evening."

"But Deliverance Hobbs
admitted to being a witch!"
Margaret's fists pound the floor
until her hands bleed.

Tears wash her face.
Though Margaret's speech turns gibberish,
I distinctly hear her say, "Isaac,"
but I repeat this not
for I know she does not mean
to name him witch.

DIVISION

Margaret Walcott, 17

Papers stack the courtroom.
Signatures Isaac gathers
enough to empty an ink pot,
all saying the accused
be not the Devil's kin.

The Village divides
like a gash sawed through
the center of the church.
Reverend Parris and us girls
and those believing
in the witches we name

and them what don't.

My Isaac stands square
on the other side of the church
from me.
I try and straddle
the hole between us
but it be growing wide.

MY MOTHER
Ann Putnam Jr., 12

Mother says,
"Remain in thy room
at lesson today."
Mother says, "See that Margaret
has the covers she requires for her bed."
Mother says, "My head doth ache.
And my stomach has unrest.
Fetch me a cloth." Mother says,
"Ann, pick not at thy skirt.
Hold thy shoulders straight."
Mother demands, "The next to be
accused will be one who watched
me as a child, John Willard.
One who was too ready with his whip."
Mother says, "That Mercy speaks
too often for a servant."

Mercy feels not well,
and still Mother loads Mercy's basket
with mending and all the needlework
Margaret ought do, and when I lift
one finger to aid or accompany Mercy,
Mother says, "Do see what thy cousin
is about."
"But my cousin—" I say.

"Defy me never," Mother says.

And I decide
'tis time Mother
learns to speak kinder
to Mercy and me.

OUR LITTLE BARGAIN

Ann Putnam Jr., 12

"Mother, I believe I saw John Willard—
the one who tended you unkindly
when you were a child.
The specters of John Willard
and Rebecca Nurse
told me they murdered
baby Sarah last summer."
Mother looks down at her stomach,
now round with a new child.

Mother's eyes fuel.
"My dearest Ann,
'tis true." She attempts
to clasp my hand.

I withdraw my palm
from hers like we play hot coals.
"Or perhaps, I did not."

Mother looks perplexed.

I stroke her arm and smile.
"My sight can *sometimes* become
hazy and *sometimes* be made clear.
Same with the other girls.

I see more clearly when you are kind
to *Mercy* and me."

Mother exhales out her nose
and says with direct eyes,
"Then I shall be kinder to you both."

MINE FOR THE TAKING
Mercy Lewis, 17

The cave of Ingersoll's shrouds me.
I pat Wilson's head
and close my eyes.

Ann says, "Margaret,
I care not who Mother told ye
she knew to be a witch.
'Tis who *we* say.
This week we see old man Giles Corey,
whose wife be already in prison."

Stead of gnashing her gums,
Margaret nods at Ann.
"For all his tongue-lashing against us,
Goodman Corey ought have it nipped."

"We also see Mercy's prior master,
Reverend George Burroughs.
Remember to call him the Grand Conjurer,
the leader of the witches.
Father sent a party up to Maine
already to arrest him."

Margaret shakes her horse head:
"Mercy lies. Reverends are not wizards."

Abigail whispers hesitantly,
"I seen 'em both.
Uncle says Reverend Burroughs
stole from Salem Village
when he was pastor here.
He must work for the Devil."

Ann be not impressed with Abigail.
"Do you think I know this not?"
Ann squints one eye at the rest of us
as though *her* words be luminary.
"Both men have been known
to *murder* wives and servants."

Elizabeth peeps open her mouth,
"I seen none ye named.
I cannot testify."

"If ye testify not and see not,
then out with you."
Ann's words fierce as frostbite,
she motions toward the door.
"Go on serving always Doctor Griggs."

Margaret adds,
"Defy your calling, Elizabeth,
and the Lord will punish you."

Elizabeth shivers.
She rubs her shoulder.
"I follow the Lord.
Pray do not send me home."

Isaac Farrar enters the ordinary
as a gust of wind.
Margaret loses breath.
But Isaac looks not on her;
he beckons me with his eyes.

Margaret be turned over.
I could melt her to nothing.
She be that much a gob
of butter. All I need do
is sashay over to Isaac
and bat my lids
and call him outside.

I stand,
but Wilson bites my sleeve
and pulls me down to seating.

NEW GIRL
Ann Putnam Jr., 12

"Susannah," I say, and a girl
twice the size round and half
the size tall she ought to be
waves at me from the corner.

I sink. My idea to replace Abigail
with this new, older girl
seems now nothing but folly.

"Ann Putnam," she says
in a voice overfull of cheer.
"'Tis your father who issues
complaints against the witches
who torture me—what a man he must be."

"Yes," I say. Susannah Sheldon's
yellowed dress rags at the edges
and has been let out more than once.

"You are as all do say."
Susannah puts her stubby hand on mine.
"A perfect lady."

"Want some?" I offer her
a piece of my bread.
No doubt she'll take it.

Susannah shakes her head.
"Cannot. Martha Corey chokes me
each time I try to take a bite."
She brings the bread to her lips
but as soon as she tries to bite,
her face blues and her throat tightens.

All the folk in Ingersoll's
stop their dining and look on Susannah.
I pry the bread from her hand.

"Goody Corey stops her eating," I say.

Susannah returns to color and breath.
"Ann, you saved me."
She says it so all hear.

UPHEAVAL
June 1692

Why uproot
a perfectly healthy
white blazing star
from the soil
to allow room
for a roadside weed?

The purple love grass
may appear somewhat
spectacular at first
with its bright-colored veins,
but it grows wide and irreverent,
knows not how to
contain itself
within the garden.

DO WE NEED ABIGAIL?

Mercy Lewis, 17

Ann flits about the room
in her white streaming nightclothes.
Her skirts pick up
under the little gusts of air
created by her wake.

"Abigail" . . . she hesitates like
the squirrel who tests his branch
before scurrying onto it . . .
"speaks out of turn.
She follows not as the others."

I say, "She is young, and she will follow
orders better than most. You shall see."

Ann ventures onto the branch,
wobbly on her little paws.
"Do we really need Abigail
to be part of the group?"

I brush out my hair.
I wish to brush out this nonsense.
"She was one of the first two to see,
and she lives with the Reverend.
What have you against Abigail still?"

"She acts like my baby sister.
I think I have a girl to replace her."

"Who, Ann? Who else has our sight?"
I pull hard on my brush.
Ann stands behind me
so I cannot see her face.

She gulps in some air.
"Susannah Sheldon, a maid
from Salem Town. She is very nice.
And she speaks well and torments well."

"Ann, 'tis dangerous to bring
new people into the group.
Forget not the lesson of Ruth Warren
the traitor," I say.

Ann's face sulks like the willow's branch.

"But of course, we should ask
all the other girls," I say,
my brush clenched tight.
"Perhaps it will be decided to be
a fine idea."

"And what about Abigail?" she asks.

I stroke Ann's head.
"She is good to have at hand."

CAN SHE BE OF USE?

Mercy Lewis, 17

We leave Susannah
loitering outside the tavern
like a beggar.

Ann says, "She'll be of help to us."

"But she's not from the village.
She dwells in town," Margaret rebuffs
her cousin.

Abigail looks down,
afraid to give speech.

Elizabeth struggles to put her words
together. "Maybe we should pray
and let the Lord guide us.
We do not know Susannah."

"Exactly the truth." Margaret stands.
She says, "We know not
that we can trust her.
She is from the outside."

"But we must grow in numbers."
Ann's hands ball into fists.

I open my lips to say
let Susannah
remain where she is,
shut out of our doors,
'tis dangerous to let in new blood.

But then Margaret blurts
from her sour mouth,
"Must we grow
with orphans and servants?
Will the town believe
words of them so low?"

"We need to enlarge our group."
I push away from the bench.

I open the doors to the ordinary,
strain my eyes against bright noon
and let Susannah Sheldon
into our circle in the shade.

THE MOST AFFLICTED

Mercy Lewis, 17

Susannah's hands nearly twist
full-round at the wrist
like a weather vane
swept up in a great gust of wind.
Her fingers arrow at each witch
Ann names, even ones Susannah
must never have set eyes upon.
The crowd gasps.

Ruth Warren stuns silent on the stand.
She cannot playact afflicted again;
none can match Susannah's skill.
Abigail opens her mouth
to cry out "Ruth Warren,"
but her lips move without sound.
Tears sink her eyes,
and Abigail tries to sit down,
but Susannah occupies
double her rightful space
on the bench, and Abigail
is forced into the pew behind us.

Ann smiles. I look away.

Margaret whispers to Elizabeth,
"Susannah be a braggart"
as she elbows Susannah's jaw
like one harsh gavel blow.

Elizabeth's eyes focus on the doors
like she herself feels chained
and examined and awaits her moment
to run.

I exhale.
This feels nothing
like a court examination
but as though
one might next see
a three-headed horse
parade round the pulpit.

LESSONS TO BE LEARNED
Margaret Walcott, 17

"They be needing aid at the Wilkins home,"
Uncle Thomas says to Ann and me
and stinking Mercy.
"Bray Wilkins suffers and they believe
'tis witchcraft what causes his grief.
You girls must visit and tell all
what ye can see of the Invisible World."

Mercy look at Ann, and I know
Mercy been deviling with Ann's mind.
Ann clutches her father's arm.
"Let Mercy travel on first.
I have a lesson to finish
and so does Margaret.
Ye shall check our pages
and when they are correct
send us forth to join Mercy."

I contain my grumble,
the stove of my anger
so hot I got fever.
Mercy grins at me out of
the side of her lips.

"I'll set a carriage for Mercy
and ye girls shall follow," Uncle says.

Aunt Ann swells with a new baby,
but none in the house dare speak
about it, for Aunt fears it will curse the birthing.
Aunt says, "I do not think 'tis wise—"
Ann stares at her and she stops
talking like she lost her throat.

Ann tugs my arm.
"Come quickly. I must finish my copy
so I can join her," she says.

"I don't want to do that healing
to none anyway. 'Tis work of heathens
and slaves." I yank away my arm.

After Ann leaves
I rip my paper into dust.
I pound my fist so all them pieces
shower round me, hiding the rain
of my tears. How can I lose
both Ann and Isaac to Mercy?

HEALERS

Mercy Lewis, 17

Benjamin Wilkins's eyes cling
to me. I toss my cloak
so that it covers his head,
and the room laughs.

Poor old Bray Wilkins
sits in his armchair,
his legs elevated,
his face a place of pain.
His water stopped for over
a week now, and like a stream
clogged by a fallen tree,
his river swells.
His face's red
and bloated enough to burst.

Goody Wilkins asks,
"Mercy, can ye tell us
what happens here?"

I hush the room
with a lift of my hands
and close my eyes.
When I open my lids
I say, "I see the Invisible World.

John Willard jumps upon
the belly of his grandfather, Bray Wilkins.
The same man I am told tended
Missus Putnam as a child.
He presses down on old Bray Wilkins
hard enough to crack ribs."

I begin to faint,
draw my backhand
across my forehead,
and my legs go limp.
Benjamin catches me.
His eyes no longer paw.
He looks at me now
as though I am a spirit.

Ann blusters through the door.
"Yes, John Willard,
whose specter I saw whip
my baby sister Sarah to death.
I see him too."

Ann's uncle, the Constable,
punches the air where we point
the invisible witches to be.
My legs jerk and my arms spasm
each time he strikes a witch.

They lift Ann and me out
of the Wilkins home,
nestle us in the horse cart
as my feet are too weak
to hold up my body.

Benjamin bounds toward me.
"Grandfather, he looked not pained.
He smiled, teeth and all,
and said his aches were released
for a spell when Constable Putnam
hit those witches. Thank you."

I nod at him, wave him well.
Parched now
and tired beyond sleep,
I look out at Salem Village
and feel like this place
calls me its own.

TOWN UNREST

Margaret Walcott, 17

Outside the Proctors' gutted tavern
a silver-whiskered man balances himself
on his tangled branch cane and hollers,
"Good folk cannot all be witches.
Think ye."

A crowd gathers round the yelling
like wasps fly to spilled ale.
"Yea," most of them agree.

Me and Ann and Mercy would
but duck away, except we stroll
with Uncle and Aunt.
They hold us to eye level.
Uncle says, "How know ye, sir?
Speak ye with the Devil?"

The wasps quiet their clamor.
"These girls be a menace!"

"'Tis true." One calls from the crowd.
I crumble to see it be Isaac.
He motions for me to follow him
after he speaks.

"These girls be innocent," Uncle says.
Aunt Ann clasps my hand
meaning to reassure me,
telling me to stay with my family.

I know not whether to move my feet
to Isaac or stay.

A GIRL OR A WIFE?
Margaret Walcott, 17

"Margaret, be you part of the group?"
Ann looks on me like I be a traitor.

"Yea," I say. "I have nothing
against your group."

Ann shakes her head.
"We are not fools, you and I," she says.
"I beg thee, cousin. Thou art given warning."

I pick up my skirts and march
from the room. I could smash
all around me to shipwreck.

"Think on this well,"
my cousin's voice rattles
down the hallway.

I will pack and leave this house.
I will go back home and stay
quiet in my house till spring
and I wed Isaac. I'll not be ruled
by some little brat and her servant.

"Margaret, that dress looks smart on thee."
Aunt Ann waves me into her room.
"Didst thou sleep with peace
  or were the witches at thee?"

I nod. "The witches were 'bout."

"Poor dear," she says.
"Come and stay with me as I spin."
  She drafts the wool between her hands.
"I am so glad that you are here.
  Ann needs a proper influence.
  She looks to that Mercy."
Aunt spits as she says the servant's name.

Aunt quits her drafting.
She sits me at her dressing table
and pulls from a box
a necklace of red jewels
liken I never laid eyes 'pon.
"Let me see how this does look on thee."

Aunt gasps and my jaw does fall wide.
"You shall wear it on thy wedding day."

"But 'tis very—"

Aunt shakes her finger at me, "I insist."
"Now come, I shall teach you
how best to treadle the wheel.
When you make a wife
you must know these things."

She lumbers a bit into the chair
but then her foot
be like one possessed and pumps
fast as a horse at gallop.
"You must keep a constant pressure."
She releases her foot and the threads
do twist apart.
"Now tell me. What witches?
Who didst thou see last night?
John Willard, did he visit thee?
Our old preacher, Reverend Burroughs?
Or perhaps Charlotte Easty, the other
sister of Rebecca Nurse?"

Aunt looks on me
like I be not only
the light in the room,
but the greatest light
in the house.

JOHN WILLARD

Margaret Walcott, 17

"Oh, he bites me!"
Ann cries and rubs her arm.

The court orders John Willard
to stop biting his lips
and keep his mouth wide.

Abigail screams
and all eyes draw to her.

Elizabeth's seizures mount
and her joints double and turn
nearly inside out.

Fingers point at the wizard Willard,
but still he claims, "I am innocent
as the child unborn."

Susannah Sheldon shrieks,
"The Devil whispers in his ear!"
She takes watchful steps
across the courtroom
and collapses ten feet
in front of John Willard.

Constable John Putnam,
another uncle of mine,
carries her forward,
tips a bit under her weight.
They place John Willard's hand
'pon her forehead. Susannah screams
when he touches her
like she's been branded
by a hot iron,
when instead she should silence.

The good folk rumble,
"Why does not the touch test work?
Is Willard not a wizard?"

I be not sure what to do.
Isaac's eyes spear the other girls.
Ann mouths, "Margaret, please."

I scream loud enough to curdle milk
and tumble into fit, jerk and twitch
better than them all.

I be lifted by Marshal Herrick
and before I feel my feet
leave the ground, my shaking bones
are brushed by the scaly hand
of Goodman Willard.

He touches me, and as the touch test says,
the wickedness flows back into him.
I stop all my rattling.

Pointed fingers and righteous eyes
hang Willard. Order restores.

Ann and even Mercy flash smiles at me
quickly between their spasms.
'Tis Susannah who Mercy severs
with her eyes.

When asked, Goodman Willard
cannot recite the Lord's Prayer,
but stumbles over it
and adds his own words of the Devil.
He must truly be a wizard.
I did then right,
so why does Isaac turn his back?

WHY SUSANNAH?

Mercy Lewis, 17

We huddle quietly down by the stream,
summer's full heat upon our backs,
only Wilson wise enough to seek shade
under the maple tree.

Ann speaks to Susannah in a voice
gentler than was my mother's:
"In court you have fit and scream,
and then when you are touched
by a witch, you are cured."

Susannah nods, but she looks
as the dandelion seedling
blown by the wind,
as though the meaning of Ann's words
scatters far from her.
I wait for Ann to repeat herself,
or at the least, to see Susannah
acknowledge that she understands.
But Ann and Susannah just smile
at one another.

Abigail pulls a letter from her pocket,
one she swindled from the Reverend's desk.
I read aloud a passage:

"Dear Sir,
Girls in my parish and I hear tell,
throughout Essex County,
are falling to Affliction.
It spreads like the fever.
We cannot find room in our jail
for all the witches. Please advise,
brave Reverend Parris,
what sound words hast thou for me?
My flock trembles afraid.
What say I before them at Sunday lecture?"
I hand her back the letter.

"I know this came not easily to obtain.
Thank ye, Abigail," I say to her.

Ann acts as if this be of trifle import,
this gift from a child, as if she forgets
Abigail and she are but one and the same age.

Elizabeth bows her head.
"We should pray for their souls."

Margaret looks at Susannah.
"What be it like in your Salem Town?"

"Oh, they be against the witches."
Susannah pulls up some blades of grass.

"Yes, of course," I say. "But more exactly,
what of the seers, how behave they?"

Susannah shrugs.

Margaret and I lean in toward her
and Margaret asks, "Well, how do thy
Mister and Missus treat ye?"

"The Shaws give me my chores,"
she says with a giggle, and looks to Ann.
"Well then, and sometimes they don't."

"Do you not torment at home?" I ask.

"No. Not so much as when I am about,"
she says. "Is that not as it should be, Miss Ann?"

"Susannah," I turn her face to me.
"Margaret and I speak to thee at this moment.
Witches do not pinch only
in the courtroom or public squares."

When Susannah answers me not,
I stand to leave and then, strangely,
so does Margaret. Elizabeth also
stops her praying and rises to return home.
"Come, Abigail." I offer her my hand.

I expect Ann to rise and join us.
I wait a solid breath. Finally I take steps
away from the riverbank into shorter grass.

Abigail clings tightly to my hand.
She swerves not. She clutches Reverend's
letter to her side and lets me direct the turns,
speed and style of our walk.

Ann runs up behind us.
"Susannah left for her home."

I look not on her, nor do I stop my walking.
Margaret snickers.

"I am dreadfully sorry," Ann says.
"It will not happen again.
Mercy, please. Please tell me
now that thou dost forgive me."

I swirl to Ann
and spin Abigail with me.
I hug Ann and say in grand tone,
"Of course I forgive thee.
We are friends."
I hold out Abigail's hand
and place Ann's upon it.
"You also are friends."

Margaret's mouth unhinges,
and she cannot speak to say
how ill this syrup turns her stomach.
She grabs the arm of Elizabeth
and causes them to take swift leave.

A ROUGH OLD MAN
Margaret Walcott, 17

"That Mercy believe she be
both morning and night."
I kick at the tree root in front
of the Griggs's gate.
Elizabeth stares as Doctor Griggs marches
toward us fast enough dust whirls
in his path. He grabs Elizabeth
by the arm, so she stumbles and nearly falls.

"Where ye been?" He looks like a dog
what some other dog stole his bit of meat.

"We were, ah, um," Elizabeth stutters.

"Praying," I say, and clasp her hand.
"At the parsonage."

"Missus Griggs needs your aid!" Doctor Griggs
hollers, but then smiles kindly at me
and swipes his brow with a hankie.
"Ye girls be missing awful lots lately."

Where Doctor grabbed Elizabeth
a red welt appears on her skin.
She runs into the house.

"Till morrow!" I call after her,
but I can't rightly be sure she hears my words.

HYSTERIA
Secret of the Girls

Ipswich, Topsfield, Marblehead,
Reading, Andover, Malden,
Boston, Rumney Marsh, Billerica,
Wenham. We see witches
from everywhere, their names
on the wind, whispered tree to tree.
We see specters all, feel
them choked about our necks,
pricking us, raking us.
We pass hand to hand the name
of the witch. Who heard it first,
none can rightly say,
just as none can rightly know
which way the wind blew in first.
All you know is
you must change sail
to catch it.

MERCY IS SENT TO MY UNCLE THE CONSTABLE'S
Ann Putnam Jr., 12

Mother stands like Father.
She ought wear his hat
and ride his mare.
Father lifts Mercy into the carriage
like a coachman.

"For how long will she be gone?"
I ask Margaret,
and she just smiles.
"For how long?"
I demand of Mother,
and she pats my head.
"For how long?" I beg Father.

"As long as she is needed, I suppose,"
he says.

MY NEW HOME
Mercy Lewis, 17

Constable Putnam
is almost too large
for his chair at the table.
Big as a bear
but mild as an old hound,
they call him Giant,
for he has to bend his head
to cross through the doorway.

"Mercy, sit ye near the stove
by the children."
The Giant's wife
tucks me onto the bench
so I sit many persons away
from her husband.

"The new governor established
a Court of Oyer and Terminer,
likes of which you'll be testifying in."
Constable's overgrown teeth stick
with food as he chews.

"Pardon, sir," I say.
"But where will the court
be held—in the meetinghouse
or Ingersoll's ordinary?"

"Not a one," he says.
"It be held in Salem Town
in the courtroom of the Townhouse.
A jury will hear the trial
and decide if the witches hang."

Hanging. I cannot carry the spoon
to my mouth. Everything
in my bowl suddenly reeks
of fish scales and rotted meat.

I look at Missus.
"I am not well. Might I
please go and lie down?"

First time she smiles at me,
her words fast and excitable,
"See you a specter?"

"No, my stomach has unrest."

Her face sags downward.
She purses her lips.
"Fine, then, off you to bed."

The room where I board is darker
than my old servant's quarters;
and without Wilson's two eyes as tapers
this chamber's black devours me.

Out the window an owl,
the king of the night,
blinks his gray-green eyes.
He cries plaintive hoots,
then spreads his wings
and twists his sorrowful neck,
as though he might dive
from his perch
and bury himself
once and for all
in the underbrush.

WITHOUT MERCY
Ann Putnam Jr., 12

Margaret slumps on the bed,
her unhappy lips pursed like my mother's.
"I miss Isaac," she whines.

"I miss Mercy," I say.

I pick at the wool on the spindle,
remove the sharp iron from the spinning wheel,
and hold it up in the afternoon light.

"What are ye doing?" Margaret asks me.

"Would smart to have the spindle
plunged into your chest," I say.

"Aye. One could murder with a spindle."

I bite the wool so the spindle
dissects from the wheel.

Margaret lies down on the bed,
hides her head under the pillow.

I creep toward her, sit silently beside her
and aim the spindle's point at her bony back,
just to see if I can.

What a bad soldier she'd make—
the Indians would be upon her
and she'd never know. I pat her back.
"There, there," I say. "I have an idea."

Margaret flips round; her eyes ignite.
"You've a plan to sneak and see Isaac!"

"No," I say. "Let's visit Mercy."

Margaret sticks out her tongue.
She hollers after me,
but I be set on my path to Mercy's.

"Come, Wilson," I call,
and know Mercy will let me in.

LET HIM IN
Margaret Walcott, 17

I unlatch the gate
and rush to meet him,
but he whoas me stop
just like a horse.
"Be anyone at home?"
Isaac's eyes dart round the yard
and toward the house.

"No, Mister and Missus be in town.
And Mercy, at the Constable's," I say.

Isaac's eyes grow darker
and more intense when I mention
that serving girl's name.
"Mercy be gone?" he asks.

"Yes," I whisper it against
his broad chest.
"We be alone."

"Why have ye not been speaking
to me?" I begin.

But Isaac covers my mouth
with his hand.

He creeps hesitant steps
to the house like he be a watchman,
but once we be inside he grabs
me by the waist.
"Where do you sleep,
Margaret Walcott?
Where rest ye your head?"

I be unsure 'tis proper
or a lady thing to show him,
but no servant or parent
or even little cousin
be round to see that I usher
my Isaac straight into the room
Ann and me do share.

When he closes the door
with a click, I start and sweat
beneath my chin.

"Margaret." Isaac sweeps
the hair off my cheek
and kisses me where it did lie.

I jitter and suppose it be a sin to do so.

Isaac's finger covers my lips
and his other hand reach down
under my skirt. I don't halt him.

He tickles my thigh and another rush
of blood jingles through my spine.
"Be this not for the night of
our marriage?" I say.

I try and shake away from him,
but he do hold me fast,
almost as in a trap.
I whisper again in his ear,
"Be this not a sin?"

"Sins need be discovered
or confessed, dear Margaret."
His voice sounds direct
as does the arrow what kills the doe.

I stare on him and begin at trembling.

He softens to a smile and rubs
his hand against my cheek.
He holds my chin up to his eyes.
"Do you not feel the nature between us?"

I look down on my boots and nod.

"Do you not care for me,
Margaret Walcott?" he asks.

I gaze quickly upward
and nod my head right eager.

"Then show me justly you do," he says.

WITH TEMPERATURE

Margaret Walcott, 17

'Tis late in the night
I wake in waters like a child.
Ann snores breezy
while I change my blankets.

In the morn I lie
still in my bedclothes.
"I cannot go to meeting today,"
I say.

Aunt Ann touches my forehead.
"You feel not hot," she says.

"I did vomit 'pon myself
while I slept."

Aunt backs away from the bed.
"Well, then you best remain here."

"Ann." I grab my cousin's arm
after her mother leaves.
"Do tell Isaac to come and visit me."

Ann nods and eyes me oddly.

"Do this." My voice be stern.

She shakes loose of my grip. "Fine."

I wait all afternoon pacing
the floor, peering out the window.
I listen for the pat of his boots,
but Isaac comes not.

I nearly scream at her,
"Did ye forget to tell Isaac
I was not well?"

Ann snipes back, "Aye, I told him."

"And what did he say? Tell me all."
I soften my sound and pat the bed.
I plead with Ann to sit down.

Ann crosses her arms,
but she lights on the edge of my bed.
"Isaac did nod and then talked to Mercy."

First I got no voice to talk,
then it comes out yelling at Ann,
"About what!?"

"I know not." Ann stands and nearly
takes leave of the room.

I fall to my knees. "Please, I am sorry.
Tell me what they did say?" I bite my lip.

"They spoke of riding and what a fine day
it be. I but stood there. It be rather dull."

The tears river down my neck.

Ann says, "Margaret, you be flushed.
Shall I call Mother?"

"No," I say. I turn my head away.
"Leave me. Just leave me be alone."

SHADOWS IN THE SUN
July 1692

Hot, stuffed in skirts
and screaming "Witch!"
some of us girls point fingers
from positions of sunlight,
others of us hide
under a parasol of leaves.
Sirens all, we choir a cacophony
of caws together.

None in the Village dare step
on the shadows we forge,
lest their name
be next proclaimed.
For as evening approaches
and heat subsides
our elders shrivel and shrink,
and we girls
grow spine tall.

THE POWER TO JAIL
THE MAN WHO SOLD GUNS
TO THE INDIANS AND THE FRENCH

Mercy Lewis, 17

I have seen him,
not in countenance
but in the blackest part
of night, in the stolen
part of my heart.
He wears the skin of man,
but his soul belongs to the Devil.
I hear his name, Alden,
as a curse.

He stands in the Village courtroom,
but I cannot tell where.

I clasp Susannah's hand,
which sweats like a horse's back.
"Soon we will be in Salem's Townhouse
facing the new court. After testimony
in the Village today we shall look
in on that new room, you and I," I say to her.

She squints at me. "Will Miss Ann come too?"

"No." My words are short.

"You and I." I let go her hand
and wipe my own upon my skirt.

I motion over Constable Putnam,
my voice raspy and pleading,
warm, so it tingles against his cheek.
"See you John Alden? Tell me,
where does he stand?"

Constable swallows, squeezes my hand
as he aids me onto the bench
and whispers, "He sits to the left
of the door. His cloak is gray
and he just now scratches his ear."

I cry out "Alden!"

The magistrates position
all of us girls in a circle
outside the courtroom.
The sun beats fierce
as a firebrand upon our backs.
Ten men are ferried out
inside our ring
and Magistrate Corwin asks,
"Name ye John Alden.
Point to us who he be."

I step forward.
"There stands Alden."
The tall man shrivels.
I net him like a prize fish.
"He sells powder
to the Indians and French
and lies down with Indian squaws
and has Indian papooses."

Alden draws his sword on me,
and the officers wrangle it
out of his grasp.
He is bound
hands and then feet,
shoved into the cart
with the other witches.
He will be examined
by the court now,
and they'll decide
if they try him
as the witch he be.

I flash on my father's face.
If only Father could know
that I have jailed the man
who sold weapons to the Indians
who slaughtered our family.

OVERBEARING
Ann Putnam Jr., 12

Susannah knocks on the frame
of my window. She tries to lift her leg
over the sill and hurdle into my bedroom,
but she can't heave herself up onto the ledge.

Margaret shakes her head.
"Tell her go to the front door," she says.

I point Susannah to the front and open the door.

"What a magnificent palace ye
do abide within!" she gushes.
Her voice echoes up the halls.

"Shhhh! Mother sleeps. Best not to wake her,"
I say, and pull Susannah into my bedroom.

Margaret crosses her arms
and scrunches her nose. "What be that smell?"

We all look down.
Susannah lifts her boot.
Dog waste plastered upon it.

Margaret covers her mouth and nose
with her hand and demands,
"What do you want, anyway?"

"Miss Ann, I brought ye these."
Susannah shoves at me a basket of strawberries,
plump enough to burst.

Margaret scowls at Susannah.
"Ye are far from home and no trial today?"

I take the basket. "Thanks.
But Margaret is right.
Thou best return to thy master's."

After Susannah leaves, Margaret cackles,
"That girl is a fool. A smelly, dirty fool."

I offer Margaret a berry.

"No. I'll not eat anything she did pluck.
It be unclean."

I sniff the berries.
Perhaps they do smell a bit too ripe.
I dump the lot out my window.

Margaret smiles at me.
"Good riddance."

CAN IT BE SEEN?
Margaret Walcott, 17

Look I different?
I can't wash my hands
to be clean enough.
To eat the bread they set
on the table curls my stomach
now that my body tells a lie.
I sit straight back in my chair
as a virgin, but fall 'pon the bed
a girl unwed.
How could he lie me down?

Under my petticoats
my skin bubbles
as a hot broth.
One of them we first accused,
Goody Osborne, were known
to be a witch
for bearing child out of wedlock.
I sinned sure as she.

I dress careful in front of Ann.
Would Isaac stand the stocks with me,
should we be found out?
Why visits he not?

I want to go to him,
but if I do then surely all will know
exactly what sins of flesh we done.
For once skin be fused,
shows it not the print?

I shake. They think 'tis the witches
torment me.
If I grow not the Devil's child
within me, Lord,
I promise ne'er to move
in the ways of the sheets again.

NECK AND HEELS

Ann Putnam Jr., 12

With Mother away at her sister's
I unlatch the door
and sneak Mercy inside.

Wilson slides to her ankles,
and she kisses him.
I never wished to be a dog before.
"Where be the little ones?"
She peers around the foyer.

Mercy sports a new frock
of blue and gold
that fits her like an apple
wears its peel. Her hair
pulls off her face
as curtains draw back.

"With the neighbors," I stutter.

Margaret emerges from the bedroom.

"You look thin as a stick bug,"
Mercy says to her.

"She refuses supper," I say.

Margaret punches my arm.

Mercy opens the cloth
covering her basket.
"Come eat muffins
from the Constable's wife," she says,
and kicks off her boots.
Mercy lies down on the divan
just as Mother does.

"Pray, Margaret, fetch us some water," Mercy says.

Margaret shakes her snout at Mercy's muffins.
She plants herself on the ground.
She stares at Mercy and says,
"Pray, Ann, fetch us some water."

I move to find us cups and a pitcher.

"Neck and heels," Margaret says.
One cup dangles from my left pinkie,
the other two from each thumb,
and the pitcher weighs down
my right side. Neither Margaret
nor Mercy rise to help me.

"What are you talking about?" I ask.

Margaret rolls her eyes.

I pour Mercy her water and she says,
"John Alden was tied neck and heels
until the blood gushed from his nose
and he did confess he was a witch."

"They stretched his heels behind him
and bound them to his neck?" I ask.

"Yea, so he looked like the crescent
moon," Margaret says.

I see Goodman Alden's blood.
I scream.

"Ann." Mercy's voice is an axe.
"Quit ye that. Ye sound like Susannah."

"Yea, Ann, else ye shall be as Susannah to us."
Margaret purses her lips
just like my mother does at me.

Mercy shakes her head at Margaret.
"Best not to threaten Ann."

I expect Margaret to rip out two fists
of Mercy's hair, but she just looks down
at her belly.

Silence holds the room so tight
no one dares even breathe.

NOT AT HOME
Margaret Walcott, 17

Isaac comes not.
I twist in the night
like a wrung-out rag,
wet and worn.

Ann wakes. She covers
her head with her pillow.
I know she misses sleep.

I pack my tapers and stockings
and clothes and such.
My home sounds as a bandage
for this gash I got ripped
across my chest.
Home might feel as angel wings
fanning me softly to dream.
Home might bring Isaac
back to me, as he'll ne'er step boot
in this place, not with all
the witch-naming folk what live here.

BROKEN KNIFE
Ann Putnam Jr., 12

We stuff into Salem Town's courtroom.
The wigged men scratch their heads,
shift their papers, ready to decide
if the witch Goody Good,
the beggar woman we first accused
who was known many years to be a witch,
will be put to death.

I hold above my head
the jagged half of a broken knife.
The metal sparkles across the courtroom.
"Goody Good stabbed me in the breast
with her knife until it broke."

Tucked deep in the back of the room,
a young man clears his voice and says,
"I believe that be part of my knife.
I threw it away evening last."

"Come forward," Judge Newton commands.

The young farmhand places the handle
of a broken half knife on the judges' bench.

"Ann, bring forth your piece."
Judge Stoughton points his gavel at me.
He puzzles the two knife parts exactly together.

The judge leans over the bench.
His eyes wind up to slap my face.

"In a courtroom one must be truthful."
Judge Stoughton reprimands,
but he speaks to the farmhand,
stares him down until the boy nods and says,
"Yes, sir," and slinks back into the crowd.

Mercy tugs my arm after the proceedings.
"Ann, do not cause suspicion.
Steal not knives as evidence."
I start to explain, but Mercy cuts me—
"You are keener than the other girls.
I expect better from you."

MORNING STAR
Ann Putnam Jr., 12

"Miss Ann." Susannah pants
and bends over as she speaks.
She grabs my arm as a brace.
"Ye did so beautiful today.
I could never be calm like ye
in front of the judges and all.
Ye work like a miracle."

"I was not—" I begin to tell her
how I acted wrongly, but stop.

Susannah pats my shoulder.
"Mighty Miss Ann," she sighs.

Mother stares at Susannah and me,
a look of disgust painted on her lips.

I look over to Mercy,
but when Mercy sees me
she squares herself
to talk only to Elizabeth.

I turn then to Susannah, a servant
not telling me what to do.
Susannah bathes me in.
I am sun and all to her.

FASTING
Margaret Walcott, 17

I pin my dress.
The fabric wraps again
round half my body.
My fingers blue ice
even in summer's heat.

"Maaargaret." I had forgotten
that voice for a few weeks. Step-Mother
ought to be fined for her hollering.

"Yea," I say as I skirt into the kitchen.

"I made biscuits this morn."
She bares all her teeth,
snaggled and black,
something green caught
between them.
"You best eat my food.
You might well have starved to death
at your uncle's, but not back here."

I slide past the table and tell her,
"I got preliminary examinations
in the meetinghouse, and then we testify
in Salem's court for the trials."

But before I can place my hand
on the door, she wraps up
a few of the crusty things.
"Here then, take them with thee."

I inhale and reach for the door,
but she holds me back.

"I will see thee at the trial
this afternoon. Judge Stoughton
doth amaze with his questions."
She swipes her brow.
I fear her swoon will tip her over
and her massive form will crush me
as wheat to flour.

"Good day." I say it sweet,
but close the door
with what little force I possess.

Three steps down the road
I yell, "Here, boy."

Ridley sniffs at my hand.
The three biscuits devoured,
he licks his chin for more.

GAMES AT COURT

Mercy Lewis, 17

Judge Corwin adjusts his spectacles.
"Charlotte Easty, many petitions
be laid upon the bench for thee.
What say you to these accusations
of witchcraft?"

Charlotte quivers not, no
speck of madness in her eye.
"I am innocent, sir."

Magistrate Hathorne points
at Abigail and Ann,
twisted as serpents upon the floor.
"What have you done to these girls?"

"Nothing but pray for them each
night, for the Devil surely torments
them," Goody Easty says.

The court falls quiet
as the forest after a rainstorm
until we girls
scream out in pain.

I shiver with a cold
I have not known before,
I know not why,
and then I see it in their eyes:
this crowd
carries the hangman's noose.

Ann ceases her crying.
I see her half-smile.
"Perhaps 'twas not Charlotte Easty
who tormented me."

Why is she doing this?
I try to signal Ann not now,
not today, but I am too late.

Abigail follows her,
"Yes, Charlotte Easty be not the one."

The courtroom stomps
and roars like a mob
of angry cattle.

"Do not play, Ann," I whisper.

"I feel pinched!" I scream out,
but the courtroom chant drowns
my moaning.

They scream, "Release Goody Easty!"
as we girls are shuttled from
a room of unfriendly eyes.

I AM THE RINGLEADER?

Mercy Lewis, 17

"How could they release the witch
Goody Easty, Rebecca Nurse's
second sister, from prison?"
Ann whines in front of Abigail and Susannah.
I nearly wish to push her into the stream
as we travel back from Ingersoll's tavern.

You know why this happened,
I want to scream in Ann's face.

I hate that I must actually say,
"Some are already against us.
We must be steadfast.
We must never admit
the path we take
may be the wrong one."
I quicken my pace.

Ann's eyes sparkle with tears
She starts, "But I—"

I fairly well run in the opposite
direction Ann travels home.
I do not even want to hear
her footsteps.

I collapse at Constable Putnam's
door. They tuck me into my new bed.

My fits must then begin,
and never a cessation.
I convulse so long I cannot stop
twitching—dazed, speechless,
choked violet, on death's ashen pillow.
A crowd gathers to witness my torture, my demise.

Ann says, "'Tis Goody Easty
who chokes Mercy.
Goody Easty's specter dances
on the beam above Mercy's head,
twists a chain around her neck."

Abigail cries, "Goody Easty threatens
to kill Mercy because
Mercy accused her in the courtroom!"

The girls all fall in line behind
my horse. They follow the path.

Except Susannah,
who never does say
she has seen Charlotte Easty.

We shackle the witch
into the jail's dungeon,
and my ailments
slowly improve.

I clearly will have to be the driver now.
I must hold the whip,
bear the cold and steer the carriage.
For if I do not,
then men like John Alden,
who aided in killing my family,
and Reverend Burroughs
with his wicked hands
and nasty belt upon wives and little girls,
might also go free.
I step up.
I wind around my wrists
Ann's slacking reins.

WE ALL SEE IT THE SAME
Mercy Lewis, 17

Charlotte Easty's led
into the Court of Oyer and Terminer,
her face not deathly pale,
but the sadness in her eyes
greater than that of the sow
next to be slaughtered.

"I am innocent,"
she says without spite.
She looks like the sky
around a star, almost radiant.

"Charlotte Easty came at us
with a spindle," Ann cries.

"Yea, she be stabbing at us,"
Margaret says.

Ann's mother pulls herself to standing
and stomps her heel—
"Our spindle is gone missing."

Magistrate Corwin cannot hush
the whirs of the crowd.

It is now Susannah's turn
to act, but she forgets.
She sits like a dumb ox.
She forces me to rise from my bench
and lunge into the middle
of the courtroom.
I tumble to the floor
wrestling an unseen force.

Abigail picks up quickly and says,
"Mercy fights Goody Easty's specter
for the spindle. There! There!"
And she points at me
rolling like a ball of yarn
around the floor.

I arrest, still as a tomb,
and the crowd silences.
All hearts seem to leap from their chests—
And folk worry do I breathe?

Constable Putnam picks me up.
I clasp the spindle
to my breast. My eyes flutter.
I crack awake like a hatching chick.
The courtroom crowd cheers
just as soldiers celebrate victory
on the battlefield.

"Is this your spindle?"
Judge Hathorne asks Missus Putman.

"Yea, that be one and the same," she affirms.

Charlotte Easty's petitions
and her eyes like the newborn babe's
no longer protect her.
The crowd has witnessed
her attempt to murder.
All yell, "Witch!"

She will hang now,
an innocent woman,
and 'tis my fault.

I try to remind myself
that I am avenging
true demons like Burroughs
and Alden, but Charlotte Easty—
why, Lord, must she be sacrificed too?
And yet I am blinded
to any other way.

ANN YET IN CHARGE?

Mercy Lewis, 17

"Well that you all followed
my lead and sent Charlotte Easty
back to her cell," Ann whispers
harshly at us and then stands to leave.
Wilson sits and will not be stirred
no matter how fierce Ann tugs
his leash.

Does Ann not realize
that Charlotte Easty, an innocent woman,
now will die, so that we will still
be believed? That all of this
might have been avoided had she
not led the girls to release
Charlotte Easty in the first place?

The other girls nod, even Margaret.

"'Twould have been horrid"
—Ann again attempts to force
Wilson to stand and leave Ingersoll's
with her—"otherwise."

Abigail begins, "Did not Mercy . . ."

"Tomorrow at meeting no one
shall cause disturbance. Understood?"
Ann barks.

Ann yanks Wilson's collar, but
he still holds his place.
She meets the fire of my stare
and hands over his leash.

"I must go," Ann says.
"Mother needs, well,
  something."

FIRST WITCH HANGING

Mercy Lewis, 17

Black, she wears black,
her petticoats like tar.
The sky is white.
I cannot look to it.
Even her blood
colored black.
I cannot see
but black and white.
Old and dead,
the tree that creeps
from the rock
wears no frock of leaves,
not even in the summer.
Charlotte Easty's
body convulses, her legs squirm.
The blood gushes
from beneath her blindfold,
from her nose and mouth and ears.
She dies slowly.
She swings
though no wind blows.

My hands ball.
I could punch down
the clouds.

There is such power
in my hands.

I bend over and retch
like an empty water pump,
for nothing comes out my mouth.

The other girls gnaw
on their nails, stare bewildered
at the body hung on the tree.

Margaret trembles.
Her teeth chatter louder
than shutters unloosed in strong wind.

Abigail opens
her lips to speak.
I lift my finger,
and she reconsiders.

Elizabeth rubs her shoulder
as Doctor Griggs
checks the stopped pulse
of the witch's body.
She then falls to her knees,
folds and refolds her hands
in prayer.

Susannah stays
wisely out of view.

And Ann, Ann's big eyes
scour my skin. No matter
what be about, even a hanging,
Ann cannot unleash her eyes from me.

REMORSE
Mercy Lewis, 17

Moon past its peak in the sky,
I wander to the meetinghouse,
crack the door to gloom and dark
and hollowness. One other figure
kneels before the pulpit.

"Elizabeth." Her shoulders
rumble as she gasps.
"'Tis only me, Mercy. I, too,
have come to pray."

I pray, dear Lord, for forgiveness.
I bow my head and tears drip
onto the dusty earthen floor.
I raise my wet face.
I fear this is only begun,
so I pray, dear Lord,
for the strength to persevere.
Guide us to banish the devils
I know exist among us, the men
who harm, the women who sin.

My hands quiver as the old
and bedridden. Give me
the strength to lead,
for I fear otherwise
we may hang
ourselves.

PETITION
Mercy Lewis, 17

He comes right to the Constable's front door,
crosses through the opening
without a knock.

I want not to gaze at him,
but it is as if the claws of his eyes
collect me.

"Never did get that ride."
Isaac smiles. He walks close to me,
pretends as he might place a hand
on my neck and kiss me.
How dare he treat me, a seer,
as no more than a girl to be bed?

"Should ye not take a ride with Margaret?"
I say, and walk past Isaac to fetch
some water from the well.

He follows and whispers in my ear,
"I have done that already,
and the ride was not all that worthy."

I turn to slap him.
He grabs my hand and kisses it.

The Constable stoops under the door frame.
"Isaac, what brings ye to our home?"
Constable smiles at me.
"Mercy, please fetch us some cider."

"I can't stay," Isaac says.
"My father asked that I give ye
this petition to bring to court."
Isaac hands the Constable a paper.
"Some that are called witch
be upright and good Christians."
Isaac glares at me.
With the gloat of the hunter
believing he's shot his doe
both head and heart.
But I run steady on my hooves.

"The Devil disguises his servants well,"
Constable Putnam says as he takes the petition.

"Good day, sir." Isaac tips his hat
to the Constable, and he leaves.
He kicks up a puff of dirt in his wake,
a little black cloud he leaves behind.

"I must tell Reverend Parris of this,"
the Constable mumbles.
"Fear ye not, Mercy.
There be always ones against
those who work hard for the Lord.
But the righteous do prevail."

GIRLS WHO SIN
Margaret Walcott, 17

In meeting I can't look at Reverend.
I feel his eyes 'pon me like I be
the next to stand accused.

Ann nudges me.
"Margaret, straighten up.
Stop looking low.
We are watched."

I won't look on Isaac neither.
I feel like I'll lose my stomach.
I put a hand o'er my mouth
and stand to leave the bench.
The tears stinging my eyes,
"I be a sinner," I whisper to Ann.
"And the Lord does know it."

Mercy glares at me and my words.
She wedges tight on the other side of me.
Her and Ann do hold each my wrists
to the pew.

Ann snarls at me.
She whispers so none else but Mercy hears,
"Do not say that we sin.

Not in meeting. Not anywhere."
She then calls out,
"Witches torment Margaret!"

Abigail and Elizabeth do sit
as wooden toys nodding their heads
like they had strings attached.

Mercy speaks in my ear alone,
"Do you seek repentance, Margaret?"

"Let me go!" I cry.

Reverend Parris can't quiet the noise now.
All the folk search the air for witches,
but I know that the only witches
in the meetinghouse be holding me down.

Ann fumes under her breath,
"I said not to act tormented
during sermon today."

But Mercy quickly quits Ann scolding me,
"I told Margaret to act as such."

I can't know why Mercy says this.
Ann's cheeks turn like raspberries,
and she appears about to cry.

"I did not know. I am sorry, Mercy."
Ann grovels to that servant.

"'Tis but a misunderstanding.
I forgive thee," Mercy says,
and pats Ann's shoulder.

Abigail screeches, "The leader
of the witches!" She points,
and all eyes in church follow
her finger to the rafters.
"The wizard George Burroughs!"

Only Mercy and me look still on each
other. "Why—" I start to say.

Mercy smiles at me as she says,
"I know your secret sin, Margaret Walcott."

I shake my head. "No, you can't know."

"Shhhh," she says, and clutches my hand.

My mouth dries up. She knows not anything—
how could she? I told not a one.

IN HER DEFENSE

Ann Putnam Jr., 12

"I like her," I say not loud enough.

"She must stuff her mouth plenty
when she be out of our sight.
All her dresses pull their seams." Margaret laughs.

"Susannah ought pray."
Elizabeth bows her head.
"I never see her in meeting."

"She belongs to another church," I say.

Mercy marches like a captain
before his squadron as we each speak.
She nods. "We are in agreement."

"Yes," Abigail says first.
Abigail warbles at Mercy's feet.
The dirty little pigeon licks
Mercy's bootlaces to be by her side.

"What do you know?
You do not even know Susannah!" I scream.

Mercy pulls me aside.
"Ann, you are the head of us."
She speaks so all can hear her.
"Susannah, think ye she be fit
to be part of our group?"

I feel damp and weak-kneed.
I whisper, "I do not know."

Mercy smiles and quietly says,
"You know. You are a Putnam.
Susannah Sheldon is not fit
to polish your boots.
Tell the other girls."

I nod. "Susannah be not one of us."
I wilt into my chair at the table.
My skin feels strangely yellow.

SECONDHAND GIRL

Margaret Walcott, 17

Step-Mother stoops to stoke
the stove fire, the sweat 'pon
her brow so thick it seems a lake
swells her forehead.
"Hear ye not that knocking?
Answer the door, Maaaagaret."

Mercy in her shiny frock
and wide-tooth grin says,
"Well then, invite me inside.
Be not a heathen."

I move aside and Mercy swishes
past me, back to my bedroom.
"So this be where ye lay your head?"
Mercy blinks her eyes. "Has Isaac been—?"

"Speak not his name."

She puts a finger to my lips.
"Ye shall not again tell me what to do
or say, or I shall tell the Village
of thy sin, fair Margaret."

"How do you know?" I pull at my hair.

"Isaac, the beast, told me." She holds my eyes.

I wish to bite her. I wish to punch her
arms till they turn black, but I just
collapse liken a tree slashed down.
I begin at tears. "I can't but sleep.
I can't but eat nothing."

Her eyes swell and I think Mercy
might also cry. But then she says,
"Cease this fussing. We are strong.
You and I, Margaret, we must be strong now.
Things be falling. The air grows colder."
She crosses her arms.
"You are not the only one
ever touched."

I rub my sleeve under my eye.
"Have you been with my Isaac?"
I clutch my stomach.

"Don't be a toadstool," Mercy says.

"So why does Isaac not speak to me?"
I ask her the question pressing on my chest.

"Trouble not yourself with what does a boy.
He thinks about only himself."

Mercy offers me her hand of comfort.

I grasp it and she motions me to lie down.
I press my cheek into her lap,
and she strokes my hair. "There, there.
Do as I say, and all will be well.
We must be strong now, very strong.
Promise to do as I ask, and I shall protect you."

I nod my head, "I promise."

JOHN PROCTOR SPEAKS OUT AGAINST THE TRIALS

Mercy Lewis, 17

John Proctor stomps the ground.
The heat sticks like honey,
and the dust of his anger
silts the onlookers' skin.
"These girls need a whipping
like I gave my maid, Ruth Warren.
They be lying like lazy dogs.
Ain't no witches among us folks.
All the jailed should be set free,
not sent to trial."
His pregnant wife Rebecca
already in jail, you would think
he had mind not to make such speech.

A crowd of nearly twenty
people cluster around him.
Goodman Farrar and Isaac
stand like watchmen to his right,
holding paper and quills.

"Sign ye the petitions
to release the good Christians."
Goodman Proctor points to the sheaf.

"I cannot pass Isaac."
Margaret grabs my arm like a crutch.

"Ye shall do this," I say.
"Else we shall seem
as liars and sinners.
Ye do not want that, do ye?"

Margaret shakes her head.
I swipe the black from her temple
and tilt up her chin.

When we approach, someone yells,
"The seers," and a few people slither
away so as not to be recognized.

"Ye girls best keep quiet."
John Proctor shakes his fancy-cuffed
fist at us. A farmer who made well
for himself in Salem Town,
with coin under his pillow,
one might think he would
keep quiet, but his voice
has been booming against
Reverend Parris and Thomas Putnam
the last several years. And he be now against us.

He stomps more, but I hear
not his words.
I whisper to Margaret,
"He be next."

WARNING
Ann Putnam Jr., 12

Susannah wades into the river,
holds her skirt just above the current.
"Ye should not come to the Village tomorrow,"
I try to warn her.

She kicks in the water and soaks her skirts,
laughs like a baby at the mess she makes.

"Susannah, do you hear?" I say again.

"Ann, 'tis right and warm in here.
And look, I see a witch!"
Susannah giggles and points,
and she drops her dress into the water,
so she is drenched.

"Ye are not listening." I stomp my foot.

Reverend Parris appears behind Susannah.
"Did someone cry witch?" he demands.

"Yea!" Susannah smiles when she ought frown.
"There!" and she points first behind her
and then to her right and then above the Reverend's hat.

"Ann, what seest thou of the Invisible World?"
Reverend Parris clutches my arm.

I stand up. "I see nothing today.
There is nothing here to see, Reverend."

CAST OUT

Mercy Lewis, 17

Abigail and Ann and Margaret and Elizabeth
all walk down the street,
their feet in rhythm
like the soldier's march.

Margaret nods at me. She smiles
as she approaches Susannah.
"Your apron is lovely," Margaret says.

Susannah blushes. "Oh, thank ye."

All the girls, except for me,
crack into laughter. Even Elizabeth smiles.

Susannah peers down upon herself.
Smudges of handprints
in cider and dirt cover her apron,
and it tears at the seam.
Susannah's eyes fill with water.
She looks away.

Susannah turns to Ann,
spitting out words.
"Where've you all been?"

Abigail is quick to say,
"To meal together."

Margaret and Abigail
walk around Susannah as if she were
a mud puddle in the road.
Margaret says under her breath
as she passes, "Susannah need not eat.
It be best if the witches
allowed her no vittles."

Margaret grasps Elizabeth's and Abigail's hands.
The three girls form as a fence across the path.
Ann tags behind them
like a little pup running
around inside its pen.

Susannah waddles as best as she can
to keep up, but our steps
be too fast. I slow down for her.
She reaches her hand out to me,
now begging me to give her aid.
She smiles like a daisy,
yellow and tender.
I stare on her.

The other girls have stopped
and watch us.

Instead of clasping it,
I wipe my hand upon her dress.

The girls' laughter
sounds like gaggle of geese.
Susannah covers her ears.
I feel nearly sorry for her.

She yanks my sleeve,
begs like a child, "Please, Mercy."
Only her strength be greater than those waist high,
another tug and she rips off my cuff.
She snorts a little laugh.
A loose thread tangles round my wrist
as though I stuck my fist into a spider's web.
Susannah pulls it, and my sleeve
falls onto the path. She holds her belly
as she chortles. None else even smile.

Ann picks up my sleeve.
Elizabeth drapes a shawl
around my shoulder.
Margaret bares her teeth,
and Susannah stumbles back a pace.

"Farewell," I say,
and we leave Susannah
on the road, alone.

ANOTHER BESIDE ME

Mercy Lewis, 17

Elizabeth and I stride straight by
the meetinghouse,
knock on the door of Goodman Holten.

I clasp Elizabeth's hand,
and as the door opens
we both erupt to shaking.

Goodman Holten clutches his stomach.
He bends over in pain and asks,
"See thou the Invisible World?"

"Aye, 'tis John Proctor pressing on your belly,
and so his wife, Rebecca," I say.

Elizabeth acts as if she sees nothing,
and I shake her arm. She flinches
and pulls down her sleeve.

I rattle. Finally Elizabeth rattles too.
Her forehead furrows in pain
and sweat streaks down her back.

"The Proctors do trample ye, Goodman Holten,"
I say, and stare on Elizabeth,

who stands there unmoving.
At long while, she thrashes at the air
as though real demons dart about her head.
Be she losing her wit?

James Holten straightens his back,
lifts his hand from his stomach.
"The pain be relieved!" he cries.

He gives to us chocolate
and bids us stay in the shade
for a while, but I tell him,
"No, we must go back to meeting."

Outside I unlace my boots,
walk toward the pond
away from the parsonage.

"Shan't we join meeting?" Elizabeth says.
She rubs one elbow.

"They will not know
when we left the Holten home."
I wave her toward the water.

Elizabeth stares at the meetinghouse.
She looks at me as though
my feet be on fire, as though

I be walking toward hell.
"But 'tis a sin. The Lord—"

"Oh, Elizabeth, one can pray
 anywhere," I say.

She shakes her head and whispers,
"Perhaps not when one lies."

I hug Elizabeth to my chest.
Her body tenses against my touch.
"You be so perfect. You need not be."

She says nothing.

I pull up her sleeve.
"These lashes, Elizabeth?
What does the Lord mean
by this beating?"

Tears puddle upon her face.
"That I am a horrible sinner.
That I must be punished."

"Don't be a fool's slave.
He that does this to you
works for the Devil.
No man should beat thee.

That meetinghouse holds
as many devils as Christians."

I slip off my bloomers
and, for the first time, reveal
the hardened crevasse of scar
the color of poisoned blood
that snakes my inner thigh.
"Reverend Burroughs's blade," I say.
I pat the riverbank.
"Stay here, where the Lord makes peace."

Elizabeth hesitates but then
crouches down beside me.

I cup water over her wounded arm.
"Don't you see, we girls must protect ourselves.
But for the first time we do so not alone."

JOHN PROCTOR SENT TO JAIL

Incantation of the Girls

Cross us not, for thou shalt see
be there power in not three,
but in four or six or five:
this is how we will survive.

For the man who calls us mad,
claims we're lying, deviling, bad,
is named a witch, his ankles clad.

DEATH SENTENCE
Margaret Walcott, 17

I arch my back like a cat
and spew from my mouth
so bright a red that some in the jury
do not believe 'tis blood
till they swab their fingers
and taste the iron and bite.
The court clerk mops up
my mess, and I shoot Mercy
a crooked half smile.
I yell at the witch in the box,
"I will not drink your Devil's blood."

Like they be offering flowers,
one by one, neighbors and kin
of old Goody Nurse
lay petition papers
on the judges' bench,
hoping tulips and roses
might stop her dying.

The jury hands Foreman Fisk
the verdict slip and he reads,
"Not Guilty."

Ann melts 'pon the floor,
howls louder than ever before.

Abigail throws herself backward,
her legs bent behind her head.
Elizabeth follows
like another stitch in a quilt.
Mercy's hands dance.
She pulls the strings
to make the girls move and moan.
Mercy wiggles her finger left
and Ann collapses on her left side.
Mercy yanks hard all at once
and seizures erupt o'er the floor.

Mercy grabs me by the collar
and we roll to the ground
like two restless pups.
She whispers,
"We must roar,
big as the mountains."
A holler with a whitecap
bellows out of my mouth.

I'll not 'low Rebecca Nurse
go free as did her sister
Goody Easty afore.
Rebecca Nurse shall be judged
the witch we say.

The courtroom freezes.
Folk cannot shift their feet,
but just gaze at our explosion.

Presiding judge Stoughton
strokes his whiskers,
questions whether the court
ought not reconsider the testimony.

Goody Nurse is asked
what she means when she says
Goody Hobbs is "one of us,"
but the old woman stands silent.
She don't deny her fellowship
with the confessed witch.
Goody Nurse blinks and gazes
out at her family, a half smile
pinned across her face.
They prod her to speak,
but her lips be sealed.

The jury writes down
Rebecca Nurse's fate
a second time,
and Foreman Fisk declares,
"She will hang."

Elizabeth grasps my hand
and that of Mercy,
and I clutch to Ann, and Ann to Abigail.
A chain, we bow heads and raise prayerful arms.
None of us can stand.

We send another witch
to the hill and rope.
What else can we do?

AUTUMN AHEAD
August 1692

Yea, the fruit be ripe,
eat it.
Things do fall.

The leaves promise
to hold tight their branches,
but their colors soon be changing.

Green unfolds
its beauty and anger,
as scarlet, maize, amber.

For all that be ripe today
will crumble
into brown
into a pile
of wither
and indifference.

SIGHT SEERS
Ann Putnam Jr., 12

Father kisses my hand.
"Off you to help
the good folk of Andover."

Margaret and I ride without chaperone
on the velvet-cushioned seat.
She leans back. "Feel the breeze.
We could be at the spinning wheel."
Margaret's mouth snaps at me like a bear trap,
"We'll do as I say when we arrive."
She jabs a finger in my arm.
"Do you hear me?"

"I haven't cobwebs in my ears."
I turn away.

The reins pull back.
My uncle, the Constable,
lumbers toward the carriage,
Mercy on his arm. I want to turn away,
but she is like lightning on the ground.
I can't help myself but to look.

Margaret scowls and wipes her hands
on her apron.

"Mercy has been blinded," he tells us
   as he lifts her onto the seat.
"But still she feels the Lord
   needs her to go to Andover."

I stroke Mercy's hair,
and she leans against me.
Shivers flare up my arms.

As soon as the carriage pulls off,
Mercy yanks away,
shakes herself out
like a dog after a bath,
her faked blindness
cast out the carriage window.

"When we arrive, Margaret,
   ye shall faint," Mercy states.

Margaret nods.

"But Margaret, I thought—" I begin.

"Ann, may I not have my say?"
   Mercy looks at me.
"What are you become: a problem,
   another Susannah? Will we have to
   fit a muzzle to your face?"

Margaret laughs, and Mercy switches
sides of the carriage so she sits
aside Margaret instead of me.

"Now listen."
She pauses with an odd gulp,
turns her face to profile
so she stares out the carriage
as she rattles command.
"We haven't time to dally.
We must work our plans.
We bring sight to those in the dark,
but we must know what it is we see."

When did she take charge?

EXCOMMUNICATED

Mercy Lewis, 17

Minister Parris's eyes
swoop around his congregation.
He collects our attention
like a chimney gathers smoke.
"And Reverend Noyes pronounced,
'Rebecca Nurse,
thou art spiritually unclean
and today art severed from the church.
Thou art alone against the Devil
and his wiles.'
The rope that hangs
kills you but once,
damnation lasts eternity."

Abigail tugs my sleeve and whispers,
"Reverend said Rebecca Nurse
cried till the tears drenched her dress,
repeating over and over like one mad,
'You do not know my heart.
You do not know my heart.'"

I cover my own heart
and look down at my feet.
What have we girls been doing?

I stand up to speak against Rebecca Nurse's
excommunication and Reverend cries,
"Witches force Mercy rise to her feet!"
He looks at us girls for confirmation.

I start to shake my head.
But Ann, Abigail, Elizabeth and Margaret
all cry out, "Witches be upon her!"
Reverend slaps my shoulder
and pushes me back in the pew,
"Poor serving girl."

Poor servant, indeed! My fingers prick and burn.
"'Tis Rebecca Nurse who forces me stand."
I stand and say it clear and loud.
All in church nod their heads,
looking on me not with leering eyes,
but as though I be strong and right.
And the Reverend bows his head behind his pulpit
as long as I call witch.

GOD WILL GIVE YOU BLOOD
TO DRINK
Margaret Walcott, 17

The cart pulls the women
through the streets,
and my fingers unclench.
I stop gnawing
the side of my cheek.
No specters fly.

They drop the noose
over Goody Nurse's head.
All's quiet and still
as the air
round a loaded gun.
The old woman
kicks her knees,
torments
as she's snuffed into hell.
I turn my eyes to the dirt.

Before she's hanged,
the next witch,
Goody Good, the old beggar woman,
one of the first witches accused, hollers,
"I'll not lie to thee now
as I never would afore.
I am innocent."

Reverend Parris holds up
his right hand, a Bible tucked
under arm, "Clear ye soul now.
Go not to death in hatred.
Admit that thou art a witch."

Goody Good kicks her heel.
"I am no more a witch
than you are a wizard."
She looks to cast spittle
'pon Reverend Parris's face.
"If you take my life away,
God will give you blood to drink!"

She sprays her curse
and he quickly bags her head.

Reverend Parris looks to push
Goody Good to her death,
speed her along to hell,
but she dies the same
slow speed as the others.

I spin round and see Isaac sneaking
glance at that l'il Lila Fowler.
First I want to stab myself
but then I want *him* to be the one
what pains. How dare he?

I wish I could march up to Isaac
and speak to him like Goody Good
did to Reverend Parris, tell Isaac
to drink the Devil's blood!

Mercy notes the rage clenching
my hands.

"Fear not," Mercy says.
"Isaac shall pay you out.
We shall see to that."

"Have ye a plan?" I ask.

Mercy smiles and nods, "In time."

ISAAC IN THE WILD
Margaret Walcott, 17

"What'll we do next?"
I ask Mercy as I dip my bread
in the stew. The door to Ingersoll's
opens, and who steps into the place
but Isaac Farrar. My jaw do fall
and so does my bread into the porringer.
"'Tis Isaac," I say.

"Yea, I see that," Mercy says.

"He can't see me eat," I say.

"Have ye a turkey's brain?
This be the first good meal
I have seen thee eat in weeks."
Mercy shakes her head
and pushes the bread to me.

"How do I look?"
I pull at my scraggly hair.
I look in front of me
at the queen of beauty,
every hair on her head perfect,
and I want to cry.

"Stop fussing," Mercy says.

Isaac eyes me then
and starts walking to our table.
I can't move nothing
like I be iced to my chair.
"What do I do?"
I whisper all frantic to Mercy.

"Isaac, how fare thee?"
Mercy smiles and tilts up her chin.

"Ye girls be stirring trouble?"
Isaac says, and locks on me
with a fierce, stern eye.

I shake my head.

"See any witches in the tavern today?"
He says this loud so all can hear him.

I look on Mercy and she blinks.

"Yea, we both be tormented today," I say.

Folk move toward our table.

"We see Goody Nurse and Goody Good
and the wizard Giles Corey," Mercy says.
"Show them your arm, Margaret."

I hold up my purpled and blackened arm.

Isaac leans toward us. "I think ye
be the witches."

Uncle Ingersoll, the tavern owner,
pulls Isaac back from us.
"How darest thou say such
about Margaret and Mercy?
Seest thou not the proof
of my niece's suffering?"

"Perhaps I am mistaken,"
Isaac says, but he eyes me hard again.
"But 'twould be a pity to hang the innocent."

"Yes, 'tis horrible to cause
harm to the innocent," Mercy says,
and rises aside Isaac.
"Thou wouldst know."

The two of them stare
each other down
like they be holding muskets
ready to shoot.

Isaac drops his weapon. "Margaret."
He places his hand 'pon my shoulder.
"You *do not* want to share company
with *these girls.*"

Mercy clasps my hand. "Leave us."

My uncle then asks gently
that Isaac make his way
out of the ordinary.

SCARLET FEVER

Ann Putnam Jr., 12

Mother burns.
The fever that courses
through town bites her
with its dirty fangs.

"Good folk from everywhere,
Andover, Boston, are dying,"
Father says.

Mother is large now with child,
but shrinking each day.
None dare speak of the baby;
to lose another one would send her
to the madhouse, or worse, the grave.

They quarantine Mother upstairs.
Only a slave tends her.

Her cry sounds like my grandfather's
screamings before he died.

"Please let me go to her," I beg Father.

But he pulls me down from the staircase.

His voice is stern. "Ann, you are needed
for trial. You cannot catch fever.
Stay in your room."
'Tis I who am exiled from Mother.

I quarantine Wilson in the tiny
back shed. He whimpers like Mother,
that big dog.

I will wait till Father sleeps
and then slink up the stairs.
I will see my mother.
I need to lie beside her crying
and let go tears.

LITTLE SPY
Mercy Lewis, 17

I stand silently behind her,
still as a stalk on a windless hill.
Abigail peers into the meetinghouse window.

I jiggle her shoulder.
When Abigail begins to scream,
I cup her mouth.

"Abigail Williams, what art thou about?"
I whisper to her ear.

"I be listening to their talk,"
she says, and looks down.

"Fine idea," I say. I join her
on the embankment. Abigail smiles.

We watch the men fastened to their benches.
They shake their heads like weeds
do twist in the wind.

Reverend's voice rattles through the pane,
"John and Mary Tarbell, Samuel and Mary Nurse,
and Peter Cloyse all have been absent
from worship many Sabbaths now.

What say you we do?" He steps away
from the pulpit and sits aside Thomas Putnam.

"A committee ought to be formed to talk
to them," the Constable suggests.

"Let them rot with their devil kin,"
says Ann's father, Thomas Putnam,
and straightens his hat. "Need we their kind?"

I clasp Abigail's hand.
"I need you to do something for me.
Remember how you stole letters
from your uncle's desk before?
I want you to take the letters
the Reverend receives this week
and bring them to me each day."

I narrow my eyes.
"But Reverend must not know you take them.
Abigail, you are being given
a very important job. Can I trust you
or need I ask Ann to do this?"

"Oh no, I can do it. I will sneak them
so he cannot miss the letters," she says,
and skips quickly down the path.

I inhale large and climb away from the window.
The sun heats my steps, and when I look down
I see the outline of myself expand on the grass—
big, black and important, taller than I ever imagined
I would stand. I stumble to think of why.

REVENGE
Margaret Walcott, 17

The sun causes me to sweat
and tremble like the old ladies.
"I can't be sure we should do this,"
I say to Mercy.

Before I can say more, she faints
outside of the parsonage
as the bell sounds for meeting.
Her fingers clutch round her throat,
choking her breath.

"Who torments thee, child?"
Reverend Parris kneels over Mercy
in front of the whole membership.

Mercy can't make full words,
but she ekes out, "Eye Ah," and gestures
toward Isaac with her eyes.

Ann and Abigail squint dumbstruck
in the morning sun when Reverend
asks them to confirm, "Isaac?"
They do nod heads and repeat, "Isaac."

The Reverend cradles Mercy in his arms
as she moans and quivers. "Poor girl."
He shakes his head and scowls at Isaac.

Someone cries, "Arrest the wizard!"

Folk circle round Isaac and his family.
"I be innocent," Isaac says as the Constable
pins Isaac's arms behind him.
Isaac spits at Mercy twitching in the dirt
and folk scream. Isaac calls her "Lying witch."

"To the jail with ye, boy!" The Reverend
points a finger direct to prison.

I hold up my hand. "No, stop, sir.
'Tis the wrong man." I look at Isaac direct.
"The specter who chokes Mercy
be Giles Corey. I see him clear."

I repeat, "Giles Corey.
Mercy, Giles Corey
be the one tormenting ye?"

Mercy nods and the crowd gasps.

"But she said Isaac."
Reverend's face bulges like
an overgrown trunk.

"Mercy said, 'He was,' and pointed
at Goodman Corey," I explain.

Constable releases Isaac.
Folk shake heads and shrug shoulders.
They settle down and then file
into meeting.

I hold Mercy's hand as she is too
weak to stand or go into church
just yet.

Isaac don't even look on us
as he shuffles lastly in the meetinghouse,
but he do know what did happen.
I should feel right good,
but I feel quite bad.

MOTHER AND BABY
Ann Putnam Jr., 12

My fingers touch not
when I wrap my arms
round Mother and the baby
kicking at her belly.

I kneel before her
and kiss her fair hand.
"Please forgive me.
I have been devilish to thee."

"You have been bewitched
for certain. I forgive thee, my firstborn.
Now fetch me my broth."
Mother sips a few spoonfuls,
but then dissatisfaction washes
over her face as though she wishes
to eat something different.

"What else may I fetch thee?"

"Nothing for certain.
This broth does me well."
Mother exhales loud as an old bellow.
"What you should do for your mother
is to end your allegiance to that servant."

"But Mercy—" I begin.

"Hush your tongue, child."
Mother grows apple red.
"Was I not on my deathbed?
A mother knows. Thou shalt see.
That servant be not kin, she be not
fit to walk behind you, less beside you."

BURNING THE LETTERS

Mercy Lewis, 17

Margaret holds the paper over the fire.
A spark could leap up and eat away
all the words. A corner of the parchment
catches to orange, and I blow the little flame cold.

"You cannot burn that letter," I say to her,
and snatch it from her hands.
"And it would not change things anyway."

Doubt descends like nightfall upon our village.
It is still summer, our days longer
than the moonlit hours, but one feels
winter coming, for even in the breathless
heat there grows cold.

I read the letter from Reverend Mather
again. "Reverend Cotton Mather,
like others in our village, questions
whether the specters we girls see
be the Devil,
or innocent people the Devil disguises himself as."
I look at Margaret. "Understand you this?"

She dips her bread in maple syrup,
swats a bee swirling over her head.

"But still when we fit, the law locks
the witches up and then tries and hangs
the lot of them what don't confess."
She lowers her head. "More hang this Friday."

"One who deserves it, Burroughs,
and four who do not, and we can do
little but stand by and watch.
Still, the Lord calls us to track
and punish the guilty ones."
I swipe the tear trailing down my cheek.
"But it is changing, Margaret,
like a shift of wind.
We will not be heard anymore," I say.

Margaret says, "We must just remain
strong and united."

I pick the bread off my skirt and dunk
it in her pot of syrup. I nod my head,
but I am not so sure.

HANGINGS

Mercy Lewis, 17

Four men and one woman
pulled in the death cart.

My old master,
who surely deserves to die,
Reverend George Burroughs,
speaks the Lord's Prayer
with a noose about his neck,
every word in place,
as a witch should not be able to recite.

The crowd quakes
as though the earth were splitting apart.
"How can he recite the Lord's Prayer?"
someone asks. Another wonders,
"Did we make a mistake?"

Ann cries, "The Devil stands beside Reverend Burroughs
and whispers the words of the prayer in his ear."
She gestures to the right of the man.

My tongue weights down my mouth,
and I am not sure whether or not to speak,
but then I affirm, "Aye, the Devil stands there."

All the girls point and say the Devil
told Reverend Burroughs what to say.

William Burroughs does not kick his way to death.
His neck snaps and his head hangs,
like a broken twig, apart from his body.

Someone in the crowd shouts, "He was innocent!"
Shoves and hollers erupt and soon people are crying,
"We killed an innocent man!" Dirt clouds
around my face as riled hooves kick up the ground.

Not until Reverend Cotton Mather,
the man who has questioned the witch trials,
raises his hands and hushes everyone
with a prayer, only then, does cease
the bickering and yelling.

I bend over and vomit. I turn from the hanging.
I turn from the Reverend Mather's assurance
that we hung the guilty—something inside me
cannot hold on to it.

PEINE FORTE ET DURE

September 1692

Beware of sturdy branches.
Not only apples hang
from trees.
Oh, 'tis no consolation
that the apples be poisoned,
to shoot them too soon
from the branch,
and know 'twas you
who made the wretched bullets!
For you who are the last log
on the load of lumber,
'tis you what crush them flat.

COLDER

Ann Putnam Jr., 12

Mercy does not answer
when I knock on her door.
"'Tis but Ann," I say sweetly,
and push open the door.

"What do you want, Ann?" she asks.
She and her room look like a hailstorm
furied down upon them.

"What can I do to help?" I ask her.

"Nothing. Leave me rest," Mercy snaps,
and turns from me. "I must think.
We have more trials and hangings,
but we must stop harming the innocent.
We must have strategy.
Oh, my head does ache."

I purse my lips to whistle in Wilson
but stop before sound escapes my mouth.
I inch to Mercy's side and stroke her hair.
"There must be something *I* can do," I say.

She brushes off my hand.
"I know you mean to help,
but just go home, Ann.
Leave me my peace.
I will see you come 'morrow."

I turn to leave.
"Will you not come back home, Mercy?
Mother misses you, Father too.
I miss you most."

"I know that you do," she says,
and rushes me out the door.

Even though he sits still and peaceful
as a river on a windless day,
I growl at Wilson.
Though he gnarls not one tooth,
I still kick him: "Stupid dog."
He yelps, and I muzzle the devilish thing.

MEETING
Mercy Lewis, 17

Ingersoll's smells of rot,
week-old bones aboveground.
I hold my sleeve to my nose.
"I seen not a specter,"
I say. "Has anyone *honestly* seen one?"

None speaks.

"This must end."
I say it bold.

Silence. The drip of a leaky roof,
the pant of canine tongue.
Abigail smiles. Margaret seems
to almost nod, and Elizabeth clasps
my hand.

Ann shakes her head.
"Have you all gone mad?"
she finally says. "We shall return
to nothing, if we are not seers.
The Lord has chosen us
to be guides, and we shall do so
as long as the Lord permit us."

"We are not chosen to see.
We have been choosing who to see.
And who are we to choose?
This must end."
I pound the table.

Ann grabs my arm
rough enough Wilson barks,
and the few folks in Ingersoll's
eye us. "Giles Corey.
You are made ill by Goodman Corey,"
she orders me like a servant.

I shake free of her
and march sure-footed
out of that grave-digging hole.

STILL SPREADING THROUGH THE COUNTY

Mercy Lewis, 17

Elizabeth stares out my window.
"It is too quiet," she says.

I wave her off, pull the brush
through my locks,
but when I listen
the night has lost
its hum and chirp,
no horse hooves sound,
no wind shakes the branches.

We hear the front door
bang open and the Constable
brush off his boots.
He thumps into his seat
at the table. I push Elizabeth
away from the door,
so that my ear presses against it.

"The committee went to see
the kin of those witches."
I know the voice, but cannot
place the speaker.

Elizabeth's hand twists the doorknob,
but I stop her from opening the door.

Constable says, "They suffer.
I think Reverend was right
to leave the Nurse family be."

An insistent tap tap tap
at the door, and another
enters the house.

Elizabeth's body arches.
Her skin pales, just listening
to the new footsteps, the drag
of her uncle's cane.

"If he knows I am here,
he will beat me raw."
Elizabeth slumps to the ground.

"Worry not, we will sneak
you home faster than your uncle
can travel. Hush now!" I say.

"How fare all in Andover?"
The man whose voice
I still cannot recognize asks Doctor Griggs.

"They have caught not only
scarlet fever, but the young girls
be afflicted by witches.
Witches are coming out
everywhere to overtake
Essex County, it seems."
Doctor Griggs lowers himself
creak by creak into a chair.

"All more reason why we must talk
to our brethren not attending church."
The mystery voice grows larger now,
powerful enough I wonder if the speaker
be not one of the magistrates.

Constable stands with a dull thud.
He bangs his head on the low ceiling beam
above the table as he always does.
"All these witches in Andover
I hear do confess to signing
the Devil's book," he says.

"Who is with the Constable
and Doctor Griggs?" I ask Elizabeth.

She shakes her head.

"Well, never to mind," I say.

Elizabeth grabs my arm.
"The Devil's Affliction
is spreading across the county?"

I shrug. "How can that be?"

A FAMILIAR

Ann Putnam Jr., 12

Wilson gnarls his teeth at me.
I drag him to Ingersoll's,
where Elizabeth and Margaret
and Abigail do congregate.

"What are you doing with Mercy's dog?"
Abigail asks, and pets the beast.
Wilson nuzzles her hand.

"I would not touch him
were I you. This dog be Charlotte Easty's
familiar." I nod my head.

Margaret lowers her voice to a hush.
"You know 'tis a lie.
Wilson be first your father's dog
and then be Mercy's." Margaret signals
Wilson to come to her side, and he does.

I huddle the girls around me.
"Mercy talks a fool lately
about quitting our accusations.
She needs be taught a lesson," I say.

"But you don't mean to hurt Wilson."
Elizabeth now hugs the ratty fleabag.

"Oh, Elizabeth. 'Tis but a dog;
your fits have sent *Christians*
to Gallows Hill," I say.

Elizabeth motions Wilson to leave
with her, tears channeling down her cheek.

"Are you so quick in your boots
to return to Doctor Griggs and his beatings?
Your home is here with us.
Give up that dog and sit down," I command.

Margaret rises to rescue the dog.

"Forget not, Margaret, Mercy be not your friend.
She be always before your enemy.
Why defend her? What bind has she to you?"

Abigail sobs, "So Mercy be banished from us?"

I shake my head.
"No. She just needs be taught
a lesson."

INNOCENT DOG

Mercy Lewis, 17

I stare at Elizabeth
as they shoot him,
a creature without growl or bite,
but only lying there in the sun.

The sound of the gun
blocks out all else
as though everything
stops moving except the bullet.

Ann and Abigail nod.
"That's the beast
Charlotte Easty's specter
rode and tortured," Abigail says.

My sweet dog's blood floods
the ground, pooling
toward Ann's feet,
but she remains unmoved.

The tears burn my cheeks.
"This be wrong,"
I say to Elizabeth.

Elizabeth with her soft eyes
looks to embrace me,
but I shrug away.

"Wilson never did but love.
It be we who do the Devil's work,"
I say.

I run toward my Wilson
but like a root snarling my path,
Ann trips me and says,
"Don't dare touch that dog!"

My face blares red as Wilson's blood.
I leave her and Abigail and Elizabeth.
I march away from them and their stench.

THE TRIALS CONTINUE
Ann Putnam Jr., 12

I knock but Mercy
does not respond.

I crack open her door.
Her clothes crumple
over her body, her room
dungeon damp and dingy.
She stands up in her
undergarments;
and, without even
looking at me, Mercy leads
me out of her room.

Elizabeth, Margaret and I
ride to town,
silent as the cornfields we pass.

"Mercy is not herself,"
I say with a slight smile.

"Leave Mercy be,"
Elizabeth snaps,
quick and mean
like an angry gnat,
unlike herself.

I don't look at Elizabeth
the rest of the ride into town.

Before we testify against him,
Judge Stoughton asks Giles Corey,
"How will ye be tried?"

Giles Corey says nothing.
His lips, like great boulders,
will not be moved.

"Will you not enter a plea?"
Judge Stoughton's eyebrows
frown on his forehead.

All the judges look
to one another and murmur;
still Goodman Corey
does not speak.
I look to Mercy for what to do,
but she is not here.
I signal the girls to stay quiet.

"If you do not enter a plea,
that by God and your country
ye are either guilty or innocent,
ye shall be given peine forte et dure."

Judge Stoughton peers
over his table to meet
Giles in the eye.

Giles nods his head.

"Ye will be pressed to death,"
Judge Stoughton says.
The courtroom chatter
escalates to frenzy,
more noise today than ever before.
Judge calls the day
as he cannot calm the crowd.

NO KIN IN SALEM VILLAGE

Mercy Lewis, 17

Though the mosquitoes
bite fierce and the hour falls
deep in the belly of the night,
I do sneak from the house.
I cannot be contained.
I crunch through the thicket.
I pat my thigh
three times calling
for the ghost of my dog,
the only one who really cared
for me in this town,
now rotting in a shallow grave.
I faint back into leaves
loosed from fat-trunked trees
and bury myself.
I wish to find family
somewhere, even if it's underground.

CRUSHED

Margaret Walcott, 17

Isaac be there to watch Giles Corey
die,
the man for whom he rode 'bout town,
petitions in his satchel,
trying to save.

As they do drop heavy stones
'pon Goodman Corey's chest
I clutch my own heart.
Why never did Isaac visit me
or speak to me after
he peeled away my bloomers?

My anger flattened out,
I wish to be back against Isaac's chest.

I be not understanding why
Giles asks for more weight.
I fear well enough the stone
I'd be bearing were the town
to know I sinned out of wedlock.

They send all us home
for the night scares the sky,
and Giles Corey cannot yet be crushed.

THE EXECUTIONER'S PIPE
Mercy Lewis, 17

My throat's dry as the ground.
The oxcart of eight condemned witches
catches in the road.

Abigail shouts, "The Devil
holds back the wheel."

Ann nods. "Yea,
the Devil tries to save
his witches from their hanging."

The cart breaks free of the rut
and journeys to the top
of Gallows Hill.

Elizabeth recites the Lord's Prayer.
Margaret nudges her to quiet,
then directs her eyes to Isaac.

The crowd's breath upon my neck,
I feel no tingles,
no power in my fingers.
The sky above layered with gray,
I cannot tell where the light
comes from or if the sun
shines down at all.

Martha Corey
folds her hands to God.
I pray for swift death,
but she gasps,
for the noose
is not quite tight enough
to break her neck.
Her body convulses like shocks
of lightning flaring the sky
for fifteen minutes.
Elizabeth and I clasp each other
in iron-bound restraint
so we will not run up
and cut her rope.

They noose the last witch,
Samuel Wardwell:
a man I do not know,
have never seen.
He opens his mouth
to proclaim his innocence,
but the executioner's pipe smoke
chokes him and clogs his last words.

The crowd rumbles and storms.

"The Devil stands beside the witch
on the hanging platform."
Abigail yells above the mob's
mumbles and roars.

I see nothing.
I want to say I see nothing,
that I am tired
and wish to be left alone,
wish to be like the field
left fallow this autumn.
I stay mute now,
but 'tis too late.
What, Lord, have I done?

Reverend Parris
shakes his head at the corpses
dangling by their necks.
"What a sad thing it is to see
eight firebrands of Hell hanging there."

Ann lifts her chin like a general
and says, "We meet 'morrow
at Ingersoll's."

"Not I."

The wind blows behind me,
and hurries me to the Constable's.
I burrow under bedcovers
as if I were among the soil
and the rocks and the worms.
As if I were all bones, no brain,
as rotted on the outside
as I feel poisoned within.

RESTORATION
Margaret Walcott, 17

Carrying the wool to town,
I feel as my feet are logs,
large to lift, and I can't manage
their weight. My eyelids flutter
and I must be dreaming him,
Isaac, or maybe he be there,
for someone do catch me
before my head hits the road.

"Margaret, ye be whiter
than a soul and feel as a bag
of bones in my hands," Isaac says
as he lifts me up. He carries me
into my uncle's ordinary
and spoons soup into my mouth.
"When last didst thou eat?"

"I can't rightly say." My tears
fall heavy as I cling to his arm.
I push away the spoon.

"No, thou must eat," Isaac says,
his voice soft as a rabbit's back.
But then it cracks with thunder:
"'Tis them girls and their witches
been starving you. 'Tis that Mercy Lewis."

Isaac stands liken he might put a fist
into something.

"Don't leave me," I say. "Please, I beg thee."
I put myself to knees before him.
"Take me back."

He holds up my chin.
"Farrars do not hang folk.
We do not call our Christian neighbors
witch. Dost thou understand?"

I wrap my arms around his legs.
"Yes, Margaret Farrar sees not."

Isaac sits me down.
"A Farrar woman sees not.
She speaks not.
She must be a good Christian woman."
He dunks bread into my porringer
and feeds me. "She must be hearty
and strong to raise me sons."

I nod my head.

"Pray well and the Lord
shall forgive ye and we shall
be wed as planned."

I move to wrap my arms
round Isaac, but he holds up
his hand. "We do not show
our affection in public."

"Yes, sir," I say.

Isaac's eyes wander to the daughter
of the traveling merchant
in the smart blue frock
across the room,
but I just clasp my hands
and bow my head
and pray.

DISSOLUTION

October 1692

Holiday ends.
Time to unpack
your bags and launder
your clothes.

Some stay on the road,
refuse to reenter
home and resume
regular life,
the sunrise-to-sunset
day of cooking,
spinning, tending, study—
pierced with the dagger of silence.

NOT ALL FOLKS ALIKE

Ann Putnam Jr., 12

A stranger beats on our door,
  a man the height and hat size
  of my father, his arms heavy
  with a young boy.

"Sorry to bother ye, sir,
  but they say you have the sight
  here, and I thought someone
  might tell of who hurts my son."
The man's arms buckle,
  and he nearly drops his son.

"Set the boy down, good sir.
Take rest. The Devil will out.
Ann can tell ye who afflicts
  your son," Father says.
He beckons me with a curled finger.

I close my eyes and raise
  my hands above the boy.
His skin looks as though
  he were dusted in chalk.

"'Tis Goody Cary beats the boy
  till he cannot breathe," I tell them.

"Goody Cary is a tried witch,"
Father says.

The man scratches his scalp.
"'Tis not Goody Obinson
that afflicts him? The old woman
half blind and all insane?"

No one breathes; for one moment
Father, the visitor and I
just stare at one another.
I let go my held breath and ask,
"Be she crazed and white-haired?"

"Yes, that be her," the man says,
almost smiling. He smooths
his hand across his son's forehead.

The boy coughs and sits up,
color pouring into him
as he drinks the water
Father provides.

"He is coming healed!"
The boy's father falls to his knees.
"Praise the Lord!"

We pray for an hour,
no words except prayers
between us.

"Not all believe we must fight
the Devil, but I see proof today."
The man tips his hat.
"My own Reverend, Increase Mather,
says to me, 'Do you not think
there is a God in Boston,
that you should go to the Devil in Salem
for advice?'"

The man shakes my father's hand.
"No devil I know cures a child."
He and his son leave our home.
They leave no scent of their boots on our floor,
but the words that Reverend Mather spoke—
those cling to every fabric in the room.

STAND DOWN
Margaret Walcott, 17

"We've been called to Gloucester
for our spectral vision," Ann says.
She crosses to stand aside me
as I poke at the crumbled logs
so the fire stays lit. When I say nothing,
she asks me, "What be the matter?"

"I can't go," I say, and feel
the scorn spread across Ann's face.

"You preached about remaining
strong and united!" She kicks the embers.
Ann's boot catches flame.
I stomp it out and she squeals
like I severed her foot.

"Make not such a fuss," I say.
I take her hands. "Isaac . . ." I begin,
but Ann boils a broth of anger.
I burn my hands
trying to touch her.
"You will not understand.
But I can't go with you.
I can't ever again. I be done."

Ann screams, a wail what rattles
the chair. I step back from her.

Her father bounds into the room.
"What be about?"

Ann collapses in a faint,
and Uncle Thomas looks to me.
I shrug. "I can't see the Invisible World.
I know not who torments her."

Ann kicks. She catches me
under the chin, and my jaw
clenches together.

Ann recovers from her spell
and says, "Margaret cannot
see or speak anymore.
I will go with Abigail Williams
to Gloucester to name the witches."

THE RETURN OF MERCY
Ann Putnam Jr., 12

Mercy winds up the path.
She squints her eyes.
In her arms she lugs a heavy bag.

I want to rush to meet her.
I wish to cling to her skirt,
and fall to my knees,
but I remain at the door.
The light behind her halos her
like an angel.

"Please help me bring this bag inside,"
she says.
I refuse, but watch her
stagger down the path
like an unsteady mare.

She unloads candlesticks
and chocolate pots, chalices
and newly soled shoes from her bag.
I almost wonder if she did not
steal from my uncle the Constable.

"Margaret be done. She sees no more.
She will marry Isaac in the spring," I say.

Mercy nods at me as if this information
were widespread as the ocean
when I know that only my family
knows of these plans.

"There are papers circulating
against the trials. Know you of *this*?"
Mercy asks me.

I shake my head "No."
Father smoked his pipe late
into the night last evening.
The smoke floated me to sleep
as his footsteps paced the floor,
but I heard no talk.

Mercy looks at me as though I am
worth very little, like counterfeit coin,
and says, "Reverend Increase Mather
wrote a paper saying that spectral evidence
cannot be used in court and that we afflicted girls
may be deluded and should not be consulted."
She lies down on the bed, a grayish color
to her face, and pulls the sheet round her neck.
"Constable's wife sent me back after she heard this.
Said we girls cannot be trusted."

"Mercy." I move to stroke her head,
but she flinches away. "We can fight this," I say.

"This is over, Ann. There is no more
Invisible World. And we should rejoice.
We have done enough." Her voice hollows then.
"Please let me alone. I feel ill."

I stomp outside without my cloak
and try to shiver off my desire
to break into a storm of yelling
and pounding and hurting
anyone who comes my way.

GO HOME
November 1692

After a fire rages,
the forest path dusts away.

It may be safe to walk,
but where do you go
when all directions wear
the same black ashen despair?

GOD'S HONEST TRUTH
Ann Putnam Jr., 12

Father closes the meetinghouse door,
the room empty and full of shadows.
The boarded windows clatter.

Father ushers me to the first pew,
then paces before me, his hands
clasped behind his back.
He grasps a pamphlet.

"Ann, a man who perpetuates
a lie is a fool, but a man who perpetuates
a child's lie is an idiot. There are many"—
he shakes the paper—"who now say
to consult you afflicted girls
is to consult the ruling devils."

Father grabs me by the wrist.
"You make me not a fool, child?
You are truly bewitched, are you not?
I ask ye alone, in the house of the Lord,
see you witches?"

I tremble. I stare forward, mute.

He shakes me. "All these months
of writhing and screaming and ye stay silent now?
Has a witch removed your tongue?"

I try to nod, but cannot make the motion.

Father slaps my face.
The sting forces out tears
like when a cup overflows,
but still I do not move or speak.

Unsure whether to stroke my head
or whip me, he picks me up
and lays me down on the bench.
"Well, ye certainly are possessed
if ye are not bewitched."

Father throws down the pamphlet.
He says to the rafters,
"Reverend Increase Mather and his
Cases of Conscience Concerning Evil Spirits
Personating Men—
he gathers forces against us
who fight the Devil for you in Salem, Lord.
He comes at us well-armed and well-manned."

SERVITUDE

Mercy Lewis, 17

"She will mind the children
and hang the wash.
She will jar the food for winter."
The volume of her voice increases
like a drunken soldier's
as she wobbles near the door.
"Out of that bed, girl,"
the Missus orders me.

I feel withered like the air
has been sucked from my body,
but I dress with haste
and begin scrubbing and chasing
the whining children. I pen up
the child old enough to crawl
by turning the benches
round the table on their sides.

Ann Jr. pinches my waist
and I screech, then smile.
Perhaps Ann will help me
clean the basin of dishes.
She picks up a teacup
and dries the porcelain.
"Thank you, Ann," I say.

Ann leans over as if
to kiss my cheek, and whispers,
"If you are not with us,
you are against us."
She yanks out a lock of my hair.
I scream and Ann smashes
the teacup to the ground.
The baby and the toddler howl.

"Mother!" Ann yells and produces
tears the size of coins.

"Mercy, what have you done?"
Missus slaps me sound
across the face, a whack
that echoes through the house.

Ann says to her mother,
"But Mercy did not mean
to break the cup. It was the witches."
Her mother strokes Ann's head,
does not look at me and shuttles
Ann into the parlor to lie down
beside her.

Ann turns back to me
with the Devil's smile.

RELEASED

Mercy Lewis, 17

"Mercy." The trembling voice
taps my shoulder while I trudge
through snow and ice
to gather stove wood.
Elizabeth stoops to help me.
"I can see no more devils and death,
speak no more lies.
I can no longer be a seer."

"You never did wish to be a seer,"
I say, and stack my arms full
as a logger's boy.

"What shall I do?"
Elizabeth's words test my hearing
against the harsh wind.

I would rather swallow
my advice than utter it,
but I say,
"Return to your life before."

Elizabeth nods as we set down the wood.

I feed the fire as she says,
"Remember that day
we tore off our stockings
and walked in the stream?"
Elizabeth giggles.
"And, did skip meeting."

"I will always remember it.
'Twas a glorious beautiful day.
An aqua sky, high sun
and a sweet steady breeze."
I smile. "And a lovely friend."
I hold her hand tight
until she feels strong.

BABY SISTER

Ann Putnam Jr., 12

The house quiets
after so many footsteps
in and out of our door.
I rock my little sister
Hannah in my arms.

Mother will not hold Hannah
or look on her. The last baby
she held was blue and still,
and Mother could not nurse it to life.

"Witches killed my baby.
Witches will murder this new child,"
Mother keeps repeating
as she pulls at her bedclothes.
Her bleeding not stopped
since she birthed Hannah.

"I will take care of you, little sister."
I kiss the baby's forehead.
"Protect you from the witches
 and devils in our midst."

Mercy appears in the doorway,
her apron clean, her hair brushed
and swept up on her head like a crown.
"Can I hold the baby?" she asks me.

I raise my eyebrows. I stroke
Hannah's head with my hand.

Mercy looks on us with a smile
soft as down feathers,
and I slowly roll the infant
into her arms.

"All of our kin except Joseph,
my father's youngest brother,
came to the baptism," I say to Mercy.

The baby purrs in Mercy's arms.
Mercy could have her own child by now.
She could be with a husband,
not minding our house and playing
scotch-hoppers with my siblings.

"Is Joseph not the one with whom
your father does not get along,
the one your grandfather favored
and gave most of his estate?" Mercy asks.

"Yes, Joseph is my father's half-brother,"
I say.

"Is it true that he keeps a horse saddled
and goes about always armed
for fear they'll arrest him for witchcraft?"
Mercy looks at me with saucer-sized eyes.
She rocks Hannah in her arms, squeezes
the baby close to her chest.

"Yes," I say.
"Mercy, you do not know Joseph.
He is not like one of us.
He does not believe we fight the Devil."

Mercy nods. "No, I understand.
He is not really a *Putnam*."

I snatch Hannah away from her.
I want to scream, And *you*
are *definitely* not a Putnam,
but instead I say,
"I need to put my sister to sleep."

NOT MY KIN

Ann Putnam Jr., 12

When I learn Mercy
told Elizabeth to quit
my group of seers,
I punch and kick and stomp
my pillow. I feel not better.
I smash the candelabra
Mercy stole from my uncle.
Still I fury. I toss all her clothes
upon the floor and trample
them with my muddy boots.
But I am still mad.

Mercy coos Hannah
on the divan.
I snatch my sister
from her claws.
I say to Mercy,
"You shall never again
tend Hannah."
The baby screeches full-throat
in her gosling torment.
Mercy raises suspicious eyes.

"Mother says," I say.

KISS AND FORGIVE?

Margaret Walcott, 17

The Reverend opens
his arms as he reads,
"Canticles chapter one, verse two:
'Let him kiss me
with kisses of his mouth,
for thy love is better than wine.'"

Feet shuffle and someone
releases a frustrated "humph."

Isaac sits among the Nurse family
and friends, those who were not hanged
as witches. They all track the Reverend
as he staggers 'bout the room,
like the Reverend were a wolf
they might musket.

Reverend Parris's voice breaks
like a boy's, and he clears his throat.
"All true believers are urgently
and fervently desirous of sensible
and feeling manifestations
of the love of Christ. That is what
this text says to us."

I glance to my left.
Elizabeth hunches in her pew,
her eyes closed, her hands
pressed so hard together in prayer
she could crush her own bones.
She looks guilty as a thief
wearing stolen shoes.

Ann and Mercy sit beside each other,
across the row from me,
but you wouldn't know
they knew each other's names.
Ann scoots forward on the bench,
places Mercy behind her
and refuses to look back.

Reverend continues his sermon
and folk shift and murmur.
"Kisses are very sweet
among true friends
after some jars and differences,
whereby they testify
true reconciliation."

But no one looks to kiss
one another. Only me and Isaac
seem able to do that.

This room cracks right apart,
like a great earthquake shook
the village and broke
east from west. Families firm
on their side of the land.
They wish ill, not kisses, on their neighbors,
each side believing the other
conspires with the Devil.
And I just changed my side
of the bench. I scoot closer
to Missus Farrar and lower my head.

INVISIBLE AS THE WORLD
WE SAW
Mercy Lewis, 17

Sent to the cordwainer
to pick up shoes for Mister Putnam,
I see six girls stretch into daylight,
released from Salem jail.
They mount their fathers' oxcarts
pointed northwest toward Andover.
Thin as spider legs,
with blackened hands
and soiled dresses,
still they walk regal.
Their fathers smile
in the way they hold
their shoulders, all of them
grateful as Sunday prayer.
I smile joyous for their release.

"They put up bail for 'em girls,"
a man with a crooked hat
and a missing front tooth
whispers on the street.

"'Tis all come round. Now those
what confessed say they were scared
witless and confessed only what

they were told—that they are innocent,
not witches," his friend with a cane
and an eye that never moves says,
and licks his lips.

The first old man motions
with his chin to me.
"Is that not one of the afflicted girls?"

I turn my head away from them,
pull my shawl to cover my cheek.

"I surely know not," the second man
says, and leans on his cane.

"Crazed of mind, that's what
those afflicted girls be, not no angels
of the Lord," says toothless one.

"What become of them?" says the man
with the cane.

"Who does know and who does care,
now that the court be closed down?"
The man without his tooth looks on me again.
"You sure that ain't one of the Afflicted?"

"No, fool, that be some two-bit girl
from the docks." The second man lifts
his cane to me with a wink and a leer.

They turn their view
to a lady on the street
holding her daughter's hand.

I toss off my shawl and walk into the crowd.
I look for my shadow tall on the ground.
I look for someone to point at me
and say, "Sinner, face thy punishment!"
But I am less visible than a witch's specter.

WHEN HE LEAVES ME
Margaret Walcott, 17

I stand too long outside
of the door. The wind blows
and clears his horse's hoofprints.

"It will only be six months,"
  Isaac said, and raised my chin.
"They need as many men
  to finish the fort at Pemaquid.
The French boats swarm
  the waters already.
And the Canadians press down
  from the north."

I clutched his arm so tight
  my fingers branded his skin.
He told me, "I must go.
I will be back." Isaac kissed
  my cheek and mounted his steed.

I stand waiting for him
  to turn round, waiting for the winds
and God and the governor
  who calls fasts and the convocation
of ministers today, to call off the war
  and ship home soldiers, not send
  them away to be captured or killed.

Step-Mother yells, "Maaargaret."
She trots outside.
"Come inside now, you'll die of cold."

Whether it be lack of food,
or lack of Issac, I desire for the first time
to put my arms round Step-Mother
and lay my head in her lap.
But when I draw near her
she smells sour as old dog's tongue
and her manner be suited to fit.

THE HUSH OF SNOW

December 1692

Cold restores order.
Shrill winds muffle
screaming, and the trees twist
more deviant arms and legs
than Affliction.

The witch hunt is snuffed.
The accusers slip
under the silent ice
of indifference.

CANNOT TRUST HER
Mercy Lewis, 17

Cold as a January snowstorm,
I rub my hands by the hearth
and tiptoe into the hallway.

"Now Reverend Hale too
is against us," Master Putnam says.
I cannot see Master Putnam speak,
but his boots smack the ground
quick and anxious.

"He now believes that the Devil
impersonates innocent people,"
Reverend Parris responds.

Ann bumps my shoulder.
"I thought you did not care
anymore about witchcraft?"
Ann talks as though she stands
on stairs above me and must
stoop to speak with me.

"I don't," I say.

Ann smiles sweetly and calls,
"Reverend Parris."
She licks her lips.

"Father!" She yells loud
as though her hand were on fire.

Ann's father and Reverend Parris
rush into the room.
"What see you, child?"
Reverend Parris asks.

"Mercy stands about idle,"
Ann says. "And when I told her
Mother asked for aid, she refused
to come."

I clench my tongue.
None would hear my speech
if I dared.

Master Putnam looks at me,
and with a voice of thorns
he says, "Be off this moment, girl,
to help Missus Putnam!"

The Reverend shakes his head at me,
eyes me as though
I had ripped pages from his Bible.

I gather my skirts. "Yes, sir,"
I say without another look to Ann.

AFTER AFFLICTION
Margaret Walcott, 17

I survey that no familiar eyes be about.
"Elizabeth," I call from the weaver's shop.
I wave her come near and ask,
"Why be you in town?"

"I come to buy flour and salt,"
she says like she speaks to a stranger.

We stand looking at each other,
none talking.

"So you are staying longer at your uncle's?"
I say.

Elizabeth nods yes and tugs down her sleeve,
trying to cover the bruise on her forearm.
I expect her to say something,
but I know not what.

"I will marry Isaac in the spring,"
I finally say, and square my hands
on my hips.

The snow falls in pieces
thick and wet. Elizabeth's hair
looks full of Queen Anne's lace.

She sees something over my shoulder
and backs away as though
a beast crept up behind me.

I turn round.
My father looms over me.

"Ye are not to be alone and speaking
on the street, Margaret!"
He snatches my arm
and looks on Elizabeth as though
she has the curse of the leper.

Elizabeth keeps backing
into the street.

I hear the wheels
and run of an oxcart.
"Out of the way!" a voice hollers.

I should grab after her.
But, dear Lord, I cannot move.

Elizabeth trips, stumbles upon
her boot and falls into the street.

A horse whinnies and moans.
A terrible screech sounds,
like a thousand birds crying
all at once.
I start to run forward,
but Father holds me back
and turns me round.

"Do not look behind ye,"
he commands.
And I do as I be told.

UNSTABLE GROUND

Mercy Lewis, 17

Ann flurries into the house
and unstrings her bonnet
with fierce excitement.
"Elizabeth be dead!"

I cannot stand.
My legs suddenly made of dust,
not bone, I crash to the floor.

"She was run down
by an oxcart.
Some did say
'twas the Devil
taking back his own."

The tears flood me.
I wish to pound the floor
like a mad gavel
and scream, "Why?"
But none in this house
would care,
so I swallow
the hot iron brand
of my anger.

Ann looks to her mother.
"The driver said he never
saw Elizabeth in the road."

Missus Putnam nods to Ann
with an almost smile,
"Well, 'tis a pity, but she should
have been more mindful
walking in the road."

The floor beneath me
opens as a pit in my mind,
bottomless,
and I know I will never find
footing in this house.

RULES
Margaret Walcott, 17

Never will my father speak
of what we girls done
the past year, for the Devil does deceive.
'Tis better to pretend nothing
happened than to admit
we girls were wrong.
But there is no lying in my father's house,
and I am not to speak
lest I be answering back.
And if I wish to be wed
I best never step boot
out of the house
(except when my father commands).
And I shall eat all what's served me
and show proper gratitude for it.
But most important of all
I must, at all times,
act a lady
or find home elsewhere.

Father smacks the table,
grabs his coat and hat
and gusts out the door.

Step-Mother sneers at me
like a dockside rat.

She drops the largest basket
of laundry and mending to my feet.
She smiles and gives me
a nasty little "Hmmph,"
testing whether I be fool
enough to talk out of turn.

I be muted now like one what
cut off her own tongue.
I straighten my bonnet.
At least no bastard grows within me.
Father's edict and Step-Mother's tricks
be temporary as a storm;
come spring I *shall* live elsewhere.

Before the hearth, I kneel
and fold prayerful hands,
asking the Lord and *my* mother
for strength.

I treadle. I mend. I scour
better than the maid.
None says, "Fine work,"
but I know what I have done.

A HANGING TREE IS NOT A FAMILY TREE

Mercy Lewis, 17

On my way back
from town
I lose my trail
in the thick forest snow
and pass Gallows Hill.
I hold my breath
as even after all these months
it smells of blood.

Ghosts wander the grounds
where no birds lay nest,
no fields bear crops,
no trees can root,
except the scraggly one
which dangled the dead.

"Witch!" I scream it
to the stillness,
for there are none to hear me.

But I wonder if somehow
my mother can hear me now.
I have not thought of her
all these months of trials;

perhaps if I had
no bodies would have
swung from that tree.
Mother, we did wrong,
we were deceived.
Pray we will be forgiven
as we are forgotten.

A villain and a vagrant,
must I lay root elsewhere?
I have accused.
Perhaps I cannot stay here.

ISOLATION
Margaret Walcott, 17

Hollow as a gutted
fish.
Lonely as
driftwood
banked to shore.
Not a friend,
not a foe—
would any really
care if an oxcart
crushed me?

POOR ABIGAIL

Mercy Lewis, 17

She sweeps the meetinghouse floor,
the look of the doe been shot
in her wide blue eyes.

"Mercy!" Abigail runs to unlatch
the doors and let me in.
She clings to me like I am
her mother lost and now returned.

"What be about the parsonage
of late?" I whisper.

She too hushes her voice.
"Betty come home."
Abigail looks to cry.
"'Tis wretched. The Reverend
be feared they what lost kin
in the witch trials will come
after him." She glances down
and says in a quiet
that does rival Elizabeth,
"And he blames me."

She bunches up her sleeve—
scars of burning begin
at her shoulder and line
to her wrist.

"How dare he!" I grab the broom
and charge toward the entrance
to the residence to *blame*
the monster himself.

"Mercy, I beg thee no."
Abigail hugs tight my leg
so that I must drag her.
I stop. She is right.
'Tis not worth hanging
to harm the Reverend.

Abigail looks up at me.
"I have written to my aunt
in Maine, and soon I will live there."

I pat the front wood bench
where we resided most
of the year, fitting and screaming
in Affliction.
I motion Abigail to lay her head
in my lap such that I might
stroke her hair.

"But until you depart,
 what will you do?"

With closed eyes
 but a direct tongue she says,
"I just never speak
 so as to be forgotten."

FAMILY

Mercy Lewis, 17

Baby Hannah curdles
the night air with her screaming.
I rush into the hall,
but the crying be gone.
'Tis almost as if I imagined
the sound.

I shake from cold,
cannot find warmth
beneath my covers.
I pull my knees
into my belly
and again I hear Hannah.

I light a taper
and creak open my door.
Ann paces outside my room,
rocking Hannah.

"Do you want me to take my baby?"
I ask.

"She is not your baby!"
Ann's eyes widen as her tongue whips,
"She is not even your sister!"

Ann backs me into my quarters.
"And thank the Lord, for all kin
 of yours find death."

Though I did not mean
to call Hannah my own,
'twas but twisted words,
I wonder what it would be
to rock my own child.
My arms pretend to cradle
a baby against my chest.

I reach behind the wardrobe
until my fingers find the envelope.
The letter from my father long lost,
but the address
to Aunt Mary Lewis Skilling Lewis
is what I seek.

I must believe that some of my kin live,
for my roots did not take to this soil.
No family tree will grow for me
in Salem Village.
I found only a hanging tree
of more death.

I smooth the envelope.
It feels as though
I clutch a ticket
as important as passage papers
to the New World.

HOUSEBOUND

Margaret Walcott, 17

Step-Mother growls
as I hand over my plate.
She removes the bread
and sets the rest down
for Ridley.

"Ann's new sister, Hannah,
must be a month old by now,"
I say. "Might I go visit them?"

Father stomps into the room.
"Does seem that I heard
a voice in this room.
Or perhaps 'twas the wind,
because no one I know
would talk when not required."
He swings a scarf round his neck.
"No one else leaves this house."

The door stays cracked open
behind him. I push it closed.

Step-Mother sits at the wheel.
"Ye are not so important
as ye believed, since the governor
closed down that court."
She smiles sly as a sinner.

"I will chop the wood."
I find my mittens under the bench.

"Ye are not to leave this house,"
Step-Mother says.
"Or I will tell your father."

I feel as to burst.
"He meant I could not
go outside *for chores*?"

"Watch thy wicked tongue.
I believe that be
exactly what he meant,"
she says without a glance at me.

She tosses trousers which smell
of horse dung on my lap.
Step-Mother commands,
"Get to work."

Six months, only six months
more in this house.

CARETAKER

Ann Putnam Jr., 12

Baby Hannah cries and cries.
I almost want to just set her down
and go to my room and close the door.
"You want Mother, don't you."

I drop the baby in Mercy's arms.
"I can do no other chores," I say.

"I thought I was not to tend Hannah."
Mercy hands Hannah back to me.
"She is hungry.
Give her to the wet nurse."

"Wet nurse left for a family in Boston;
conditions are better there."
I roll the infant back to Mercy.

Mercy bounces Hannah,
and she stops crying like
Mercy cast a spell upon her.

"Mother *and* Father stricken.
I pray we don't lose them both."
I lean against the table.

Mercy holds the baby in one arm
and chops the legs off a chicken
with her free hand.

"I would be sent to live with Uncle John.
My brothers and sisters
would be scattered all about," I say.

White feathers gather like piles of snow
on either side of Mercy.

"Yes," Mercy says.
Her eyes never rise from her work.

My chest heaves.
I huff and fall into a chair.
"That would be dreadful
to lose our house and farm."
I touch my forehead and say,
"I might have a fever."

"Ann!" Mother screams,
loud and troubled.

"Mercy," I plead.
"I have been tending her and Father
for two days. I *must* rest."

"What other help do we have?"
Mercy asks. Her eyes are the bull's
right before he runs.

"None. They are helping repair
the meetinghouse so that it won't
be dreadful cold every Sabbath.
Father promised the Reverend
that he would—"

She holds up her hand.
"Just go."

"The other little ones are napping,"
I say, and limp to my bedroom.

A scream from the nursery
feels like knives in my side.
I quicken my steps.

"Ann!" Mother hollers again.

I bury my head under the pillow.

GOOD-BYE, SALEM
Mercy Lewis, 17

The house creaks farewell.
Gales blow up snow
as sand pebbles are moved
by the tides.
The gate bang, bangs
in the wind, sounds
as if it might fly off its hinges.

Morning cracks over the trees
orange and gold.

All my dresses on,
the blue atop the brown,
each step, I feel how heavy it be.

I grasp the envelope
addressed Aunt Mary Lewis Skilling Lewis
written by Father so many years back.
Pray she will take me in,
for there is no loyalty as strong as family.

The snow falls fresh this morning,
I track no ashes of the Invisible World.
In New Hampshire I start anew.

THE REAL GIRLS
AND WHAT
HAPPENED TO THEM

in order of appearance

MERCY LEWIS *(age 17)* In 1692 the real Mercy Lewis was indeed seventeen and did serve in Thomas Putnam's home. Mercy legally accused fifty-four people of witchcraft and gave formal testimony at twelve public examinations or trials. After the crisis of 1692 Mercy moved to Greenland, New Hampshire, to live near her aunt. She bore a bastard child in 1695 and later married the presumed father of her child, Charles Allen. She and Charles then moved to Boston.

MARGARET WALCOTT *(age 17)* Margaret Walcott is based upon the real Mary Walcott. Mary was involved in sixty-nine legal complaints and testified twenty-eight times. She married Isaac Farrar in 1696 and bore him seven children. They raised their family in his hometown of Ashford, Connecticut.

ANN PUTNAM JR. *(age 12)* The real twelve-year-old Ann Putnam Jr. made fifty-three legal complaints and formally testified twenty-eight times. One of the last girls to end her accusations and testimony, Ann is recorded as having testified up until May 1693. Her parents died within two weeks of each other in 1699, and Ann was left to care for her seven siblings. When Ann joined the Village Church in 1706, she begged forgiveness and declared that Satan had deceived her into accusing people of witchcraft. Ann was the only accuser known to account for her actions in the crisis. Ann Putnam Jr. died unmarried in 1715.

BETTY PARRIS *(age 8)* The real Betty Parris signed only three legal complaints. She never testified. In March 1692, Reverend Parris moved his daughter to the home of his friend Stephen Sewall, in hopes that her torments might ease. Betty Parris married Benjamin Barron in 1710. She raised five children and died at age seventy-six.

ABIGAIL WILLIAMS *(age 12)* The real Abigail Williams lived with her uncle Reverend Parris during the crisis of 1692. She and Betty Parris, her cousin, were the first two afflicted girls. Abigail accused forty-one people of being witches and testified in seven cases. What became of the real Abigail Williams is not part of the historical record. It is surmised that she died unmarried.

ELIZABETH HUBBARD *(age 17)* The real "Betty" Hubbard formally accused forty-one people of witchcraft. She testified in thirty-two cases. After the crisis Betty moved to Gloucester, probably to live with one of Dr. Griggs's married children. There she met and married John Bennett. Betty Hubbard's death date is unknown.

SUSANNAH SHELDON *(age 18)* The real Susannah Sheldon signed twenty-four legal complaints but was recorded to have testified in only three cases. After her participation in the Salem trials, she moved to Providence, Rhode Island. But because Susannah was "a person of Evil fame," the Providence town council warned her out of town. What happened to her after that is not certain, though it is likely that she went mad. It is believed that she died unmarried before 1697.

THE REAL PEOPLE
THE GIRLS ACCUSE

in order of first mention in the book

TITUBA was a slave of Reverend Parris's from Barbados. She was the first witch accused. It was thought that she taught the girls some folk magic. She also baked a "witch cake" using Betty's and Abigail's urine to test if the girls were bewitched. Baking the cake fortified the notion that Tituba was herself a witch. Upon examination Tituba confessed to practicing witchcraft in elaborate detail. Her confession in many ways fueled the large-scale witch hunt. Tituba was not released from jail until May 1693 because prisoners had to pay for their imprisonment, and Reverend Parris would not settle her jail debt. Reverend Parris sold her to an unidentified person who paid her prison tab.

SARAH GOOD and her daughter were reduced to begging. Sarah was surly and therefore long considered a witch. She was one of the first three witches accused. She was hanged July 19, 1692.

SARAH OSBORNE, one of the first three witches accused, married Robert Prince, an in-law of Thomas Putnam, in 1662. After Prince died, Sarah Osborne "lived in sin" with her indentured servant, Alexander Osborne, and then married him in 1677. She then tried to disinherit the two sons she had with Prince (who were the cousins of Thomas Putnam). At the time of her accusal, Sarah was ailing and senile. She died in prison on May 10, 1692.

ELIZABETH PROCTOR (in the book REBECCA PROCTOR) was also easily accepted as a witch because her grandmother Goody Burt had been accused of witchcraft thirty years before Elizabeth. Her husband, John, held a license to sell liquor from their home, but Elizabeth often was the one to serve it. Her husband tried to defend her in court during examination and was a vocal opponent of the witch hunt. He became accused of witchcraft. Ruth Warren, whose real name was Mary Warren, was their servant. The court pronounced Elizabeth guilty, but she begged for a reprieve as she was pregnant. The court granted her request and spared her the noose. Her husband was not so fortunate.

REBECCA NURSE was seventy-one, ailing, and partially deaf at the time of her accusal. Rebecca Nurse had eight children, and the Nurse family was established as one of the prosperous families with over three hundred acres of land by 1692. She was known for her piety and was a full member of the Salem Town church. Her husband formed part of the Anti-Reverend Parris committee, and he had been in a land dispute with Nathaniel Putnam in the 1670s. The witchcraft accusation against Rebecca Nurse aroused more protest than that against any other witchcraft victim. She was hanged on July 19, 1692.

MARTHA COREY was publicly skeptical about the existence of witches in Salem Village. The fourth person accused, Martha was the first Salem Village church member accused. Though she became pious, her reputation was tainted because she had given birth to an illegitimate child, a mulatto. Her husband was Giles Corey. She was hanged September 22, 1692.

MARY WARREN (in the book RUTH WARREN) was John and Elizabeth Proctor's maid. When she became afflicted, John whipped her until she claimed she no longer saw witches. She tacked her recantation onto the meetinghouse door. Mary was then accused of witchcraft and at her examination she broke into fit, again deciding to be one of the afflicted girls. She implicated both John and Elizabeth, among a long list of other known "witches" while in jail. Mary Warren was released but returned to a household of five children and no master or mistress. The sheriff had seized all of the Proctors' belongings because an accused witch's estate always became forfeit.

SARAH CLOYSE was a sister of Rebecca Nurse and the sister-in-law of Mercy Lewis's paternal aunt. She was a member of the Salem Village church. Skeptical about the witch accusations and angered over the imprisonment of Rebecca, she marched out of the meetinghouse in protest of the sermon "Christ Knows How Many Devils There Are in His Churches, and Who They Are." After questioning the girls and then fainting during her formal examination in April 1692, Sarah Cloyse was assigned to the larger Boston jail. Rebecca Nurse was hanged on July 19, 1692, and Sarah and Mary Easty (Charlotte Easty in the book), the two surviving sisters, petitioned the court to hear evidence both *for* and against the accused. They petitioned for a fair trial. The petition, though beautifully written, impacted nothing. It did not spare Mary Easty the noose. Fortunately for Sarah, her case never went to court. She was released from jail in January 1693.

BRIDGET BISHOP had been accused of witchcraft twelve years earlier. She lived in Salem Town and was known to the girls only by reputation. Rumored to have bewitched to death children and her first husband, she was the first witch to hang, on June 10, 1692.

DELIVERANCE HOBBS, at her examination, confessed to signing the Devil's book. She later tried to deny her confession, and the girls once again became afflicted by her. Deliverance wound up implicating Bridget Bishop in order to save herself.

GILES COREY, prosperous eighty-year-old farmer and husband to Martha Corey, had a reputation for aggression. He was brought to court in 1675 for beating a manservant to death. Giles testified against his own wife at her examination and then soon was accused himself. He would not enter a plea and stood mute at his trial. He was sentenced to peine forte et dure; heavy stones would press him into entering a plea or crush him to death. He died September 19, 1692.

REVEREND GEORGE BURROUGHS was considered by the accusers to be the Grand Conjurer, the leader of the witches. According to the girls, he oversaw meetings that all the witches attended in the pasture beside the meetinghouse. He was the Salem Village minister from 1680 to 1683, and then returned to Maine after having disagreements with Thomas Putnam and his allies. Mercy Lewis served in his house up north when she was eight years old and recently orphaned. She witnessed him abuse two wives and probably was also abused by him. Reverend Burroughs was brought back to Salem Village as a prisoner. On August 19, 1692, the date of his execution, he recited the Lord's Prayer without a mistake just before he was hanged, a feat thought to be impossible for a witch. The crowd screamed and feared that an innocent man was being put to death. But Reverend Cotton Mather, who was often a strong opponent of the witch trials, convinced everyone at Gallows Hill that George Burroughs was indeed a wizard and as such deserved to hang.

NEHEMIAH ABBOTT was a Topsfield weaver in his midtwenties whose specter Ann Jr. declares to have seen. But after a formal examination and Mercy's decisive declaration that "it is not the man," Ann recanted her public statements, and Nehemiah Abbott was let go free without serving any jail time and without being sentenced. This was the only time in the witchcraft trials that has been recorded where someone was brought to formal sentencing but the accusers publicly disagreed and then released the accused as innocent.

JOHN WILLARD tended Ann Putnam Sr. when she was a child. Ann Putnam Jr. first saw Willard's specter whip her sister Sarah to death. Sarah died as an infant in 1689. Willard then sought prayer and counsel with some of his family, the Wilkinses, but after he visited them old Bray Wilkins could not urinate and suffered tremendous pain. Seventeen-year-old Daniel fell ill and died. John Willard was blamed for these incidents, and the girls' spectral sight confirmed the families' assumptions. Willard anticipated his arrest and fled. He was captured in Groton on May 16, 1692. John Willard was hanged August 19, 1692.

JOHN ALDEN had ties to Maine and the frontier wars. He was a wealthy mariner from a prominent family that came over on the *Mayflower* and was a member of the Boston Church. The famous quote about John Alden, generally attributed to Ann Putnam Jr. but in the book attributed to Mercy Lewis was, "There stands Alden, a bold fellow with his hat on before the judges. He sells powder and shot to the Indians and French and lies with the Indian squaws and has Indian papooses." And there was indeed testimonial evidence by those who knew Alden from the frontier wars that this "gossip" was true. Because John Alden had enough money, he paid off his jailers and escaped. By the time he was recovered, the witch trials were over, and the court cleared Alden by proclamation.

JOHN PROCTOR was the husband of Elizabeth Proctor (Rebecca Proctor in the book). Native to Ipswich, he moved to Salem Village in his thirties and prospered not only as a farmer but also as a tavern keeper and entrepreneur. John spoke loudly against the witch hunt from its inception. He whipped his maid Mary Warren (Ruth Warren in the book) into recanting her spectral sight. John and his wife were both accused of witchcraft in the spring of 1692, she first. John Proctor was hanged at Gallows Hill August 19, 1692.

MARY EASTY (in the book CHARLOTTE EASTY) was a sister to both Rebecca Nurse and Sarah Cloyse, and apparently the most intelligent and pious of the lot. Formal complaints that she was indeed a witch were issued against Easty on April 21, 1692; and she was sentenced to join her sisters in the Boston jail. On May 18, 1692, an unprecedented event occurred: she was released from jail for three days, but when the girls suffered most terrible fits, Mary Easty was returned to incarceration. Mary wrote an eloquent petition after she was sentenced to die, not to spare her own life, but so that the others yet accused might receive more just and equitable trials. Mary Easty was hanged September 22, 1692.

SAMUEL WARDWELL was a forty-nine-year-old carpenter from New Hampshire who confessed that he had become "discontented" and had "foolishly" become involved with fortune-telling and the "black man" (the Devil). Interestingly, Samuel had been integral in convincing other people to confess during their examinations. Samuel recanted his confession to the grand jury, but they believed his initial statements and sentenced him to die. He was hanged September 22, 1692.

∽

IN THE END, nineteen people were hanged (fourteen women and five men). One man was pressed to death. Three women and several infants died in jail, and more than 144 people had legal action brought against them.

AUTHOR'S NOTE

The idea to write a book about the Salem witch trials was offered to me by a friend. I went online and off to the library to see if I could find something intriguing, something I could invest in or relate to about the project. What struck me immediately in the research was the idea that the teen girls of Salem Village managed to become the most powerful people in town during the 1692 witch trials. Especially since the girls found power through madness and wrongdoing, I was hooked right then and knew I wanted to write their story. History revealed a story of group dynamics within the larger community and, I imagined, within the girl clique itself. The tale that unfolded seemed so timeless and incredibly relevant today. Here was a story of the pitfalls of peer pressure, gossip and girl group dynamics that led to false empowerment.

The greatest mystery of the Salem witch trials is what motivated the girls to name people witches. As far as we know today, no precise answer was ever given. The girls were silenced, not allowed to explain themselves, a sort of ultimate disempowerment. *Wicked Girls* provides fictional backstories for and gives fictional voices to some of the real girls whose testimony named people witches and ultimately led to nineteen hangings in 1692.

The afflicted girls' "bewitchment" was what the Village elders interpreted the girls' fits as being. Their afflictions just as easily could have been declared religious fervor, and in fact similar youth behavior in the eighteenth century led to the Great Revival. It is hard to imagine today, but people believed in witches much as they believed in God and Satan. Times were hard, and many families were losing fathers, sons, uncles, mothers, daughters, babies and livestock to war, Indian raids, famine and illness. Settlers in the late seventeenth century needed an explanation for this suffering and loss, and witches doing Satan's bidding seemed logical and reasonable to the Puritans. But this still did not fully explain why the girls accused more than 220 people (and a great number of them folk whom the girls themselves had never met) of being witches.

Many theories exist about the girls' actions. Some of the medical theories include that the girls suffered from a psychological hysteria, a sort of posttraumatic stress disorder in response to Indian attacks and nearly two decades of the frontier war; that the girls had a mental breakdown as a result of watching their families slaughtered by Indian attacks

and war. Another theory is that they contracted con-
vulsive ergotism caused by eating fungus-infected rye
bread. In other words, they ate old bread and it made
them "high" and caused them to see visions. This theory is not widely accepted. A final medical theory is
that they caught an epidemic of bird-borne encepha-
litis lethargic, a sort of flu that made them hysterical.
Many historians are inclined to believe that the cause
for the girls' behavior was not biological and feel that
their motivation was jealousy, spite and a need for
attention—that the girls were simply acting. A more
sociopolitical explanation for their behavior is that
those affiliated with Salem Town in general, the new
bourgeois (and specifically those related to the Por-
ter family), fell into conflict with the landed gentry in
Salem Village headed by the Putnam family. A number of issues dealing with land, inheritance and the
reverend selected for Salem Village created a sort of
feud between the two major families settled in the
Village. However, whatever the theory, almost all the
historians seem to agree that it is likely that the first
fits of Betty and Abigail were *not* intentional.

Wicked Girls combines some of these theories, but the
basic premise I fictionally represent is that the accusers
"faked" their affliction and knew what they were doing.
Girls had no voice in a Puritan society, and that lack of
power may have constricted them to the point of hysteria. Life was very hard, and any opportunity for relief

from daily burdens would be tempting. This book also tries to incorporate some of the socioeconomic reasoning and the ways in which war contributed to the girls' behavior. It should be noted that not all accusers were girls. Many adult men and women accused their neighbors of being witches. Oftentimes the people accused would confess to being witches, which may seem ridiculous. But that was because, although a confession locked a "witch" in jail, without exception it spared her/him the hangman's noose. Confessions obviously strengthened the girls' accusations and spurred on the hunt.

As this is a work of fiction, for storytelling purposes and to help distinguish between characters, certain names and accounts have been changed, amended or altered with the intention to best serve the book as a whole. I have attempted to do this with as much integrity and authenticity as possible. Research for historical fiction is challenging because sources are often in conflict. I read as long and as much as I could and I traveled to Massachusetts. At the Boston Museum of Fine Arts, I examined furniture, porringers and articles from the seventeenth century. I visited Danvers, Massachusetts (what used to be Salem Village), walked the Nurse family farm and breathed the air. Step away from the wax witch museum in Salem, and you can smell the ghosts. The spirits remind us all: do not forget what happened here.

SHOULD YOU WISH TO EXPLORE FURTHER

Here is a Partial List of Sources Used for *Wicked Girls*

ARONSON, MARC.
Witch Hunt: Mysteries of the Salem Witch Trials.
New York: Simon & Schuster Children's Publishing
Division, 2003.

BOYER, PAUL, AND STEPHEN NISSENBAUM.
Salem Possessed: The Social Origins of Witchcraft.
Cambridge, MA: Harvard University Press, 1974.

BOYER, PAUL, AND STEPHEN NISSENBAUM, EDS.
*Salem-Village Witchcraft: A Documentary Record of Local
Conflict in Colonial New England.* Boston: Northeastern
University Press, 1972.

HILL, FRANCES.
*A Delusion of Satan: The Full Story of the Salem Witch
Trials.* New York: Doubleday, 1995.

NORTON, MARY BETH.
In the Devil's Snare: The Salem Witchcraft Crisis of 1692.
New York: Random House, 2003.

ROACH, MARILYNNE K.
The Salem Witch Trials: A Day-by-Day Chronicle of a Community Under Siege. Lanham, MA: The Rowman & Littlefield Publishing Group, 2004.

SPEARE, ELIZABETH GEORGE.
The Witch of Blackbird Pond. New York: Random House, 1958.

STARKEY, MARION L.
The Devil in Massachusetts: A Modern Enquiry into the Salem Witch Trials. New York: Random House, 1949.

www.etext.virginia.edu/salem/witchcraft/

www.salemwitchtrials.com

www.17thc.us/